MW00744609

The Newsboy Partners; Or, Who Was Dick Box?

by Frank V. Webster

Copyright © 8/5/2015
Jefferson Publication

ISBN-13: 978-1515369707

Printed in the United States of America

All rights reserved. No part of this book may be reprinted or reproduced or utilized in any form or by any electronic, mechanical, or other means, now known or hereafter invented, including photocopying and recording, or in any form of storage or retrieval system, without prior permission in writing from the publisher.'

Contents

CHAPTER I

JIMMY IS IN LUCK

"Wuxtry! Wuxtry! Full account of de big f-i-r-e! Here ye are! Wuxtry! *Woild, Joinal, Sun, Telegram*! Here ye are, mister! Git de latest wuxtry! Wuxtry! Wuxtry!"

Jimmy Small was only one of a dozen newsboys crying the same thing in City Hall Park, New York. The lads, ragged little chaps, were rushing at all in whom they saw possible customers, thrusting the papers in their very faces, a fierce rivalry taking place whenever two of the boys reached the same man at the same time. But of all who cried none shouted louder than this same Jimmy Small, and none was more active in rushing here and there with papers.

"Wuxtry! Wuxtry!" yelled Jimmy, for that was how he and the other boys pronounced the word "Extra."

"What's the extra about?" asked a well-dressed man, stopping Jimmy.

"Wuxtry! Big fire! Dozen people burned to death! Here ye are! Wuxtry! Full account of de big f-i-r-e!"

Jimmy could not stop long to talk. He must sell papers. He snatched one from the bundle under his arm, thrust it into the man's hand, took the nickel the customer gave him, handed the man four pennies in change, and all the while was yelling at the top of his voice his war-cry:

"Wuxtry! Wuxtry!"

Jimmy had secured his bunch of papers from one of the delivery wagons on Park Row—Newspaper Row, as it is sometimes called. He had dashed across the park toward Broadway, selling as he ran. He wanted to reach a certain corner at Broadway and Barclay Street, where he could be sure of finding many customers who would buy papers on their way to take the ferry over to New Jersey. Jimmy usually made that corner his headquarters.

As he hurried on he was stopped several times by men who, attracted by his loud shouts, wanted to buy papers to see what the extra was about. As it happened, there had been a disastrous fire in New York that day in which a number of per-

[Transcriber's note: page 3 missing from book]
[Transcriber's note: page 4 missing from book]

"Well, I ain't yer son. Ner I ain't no signpost either. D'ye want a pape?"

"I don't know. Perhaps I might take one," was the answer in drawling tones. "Are you selling papers?"

"Naw, I'm here fer me health. De doctor said I had t' stand here t' git fresh air," replied Jimmy with contempt in his tones, for he saw that the young man was from the country, unused to city ways, and, as a boy who had lived in New York all his life, Jimmy had not much use for country folks.

"You're something of a joker, aren't you?" asked the young man, good humor showing in his blue eyes. He did not seem to be offended at Jimmy's answer.

"Naw, I'm a newsie. Want a pape? *Sun, Woild, Joinal*? Wuxtry! All about de big fire!"

"Which is the best paper?" asked the young man with a smile.

"Aw, g'wan! T'ink I'm going t' play favorites? Dey is all alike t' me. One's de same as de udder. I ain't goin' t' knock any of 'em. I makes me livin' by sellin' 'em all, dat's what!"

"Then I guess I'll take a *Sun*. But could you tell me the way to the Brooklyn Bridge? I'm a stranger in New York."

"Oh, I kin see dat all right enough," replied Jimmy with a little kindlier feeling toward the man, now that he had proved to be a customer. "Youse from de country all right."

"How can you tell that?"

"'Cause youse talks so slow. Folks here ain't got time t' waste so much talk over deir woids. Ye got t' hustle in N'York."

"I believe you, from what little I have seen. You are right, I am from the country, and I'm on my way to visit an aunt in Brooklyn. I thought I'd walk over the bridge, for I've read a lot about it."

"Well, go up one block," said Jimmy, pointing toward Park Place, "den cut t'rough City Hall Park by de side of de post-office here an' foller de crowd. Youse can't miss it. But youse wants t' look out."

"What for?"

"If ye gits in de push youse'll be squeezed t' death. It's an awful mob dat goes t' Brooklyn dis time o' day."

"Well, I'll be careful. Do you live around here?"

"Who, me? Oh, yes, I lives around here," and Jimmy, with a wave of his hand, included nearly the whole of New York.

"What's your name?"

"Say, who are youse, anyhow?" inquired the newsboy, suddenly suspicious.

"My name is Joshua Crosscrab, and I'm from Newton, Vermont," replied the young man, still good-natured.

"Aw, I mean who be ye? Be youse a detective, er from some society what takes up kids fer sellin' papes on de street?"

"No, I'm not a detective. What makes you think so?"

"'Cause youse asks so many questions."

"I am interested. I never was in New York before, and I see so many things that are strange that I want to know about them. Up our way we believe in getting acquainted, so I thought I'd try it here. Every one I talked to, though, seemed to think I was a swindler, I guess."

"Dat's right. Youse has t' be careful who youse talk to in N'York," said Jimmy with a comical air of wisdom.

"But you haven't told me your name yet," persisted Mr. Crosscrab.

"Sure youse ain't none of them children sasiety detectives?" asked the newsboy.

"Sure. I'll give you my promise."

"Well, me name is Jimmy Small. Here ye are, sir! Paper! Wuxtry! All about de big fire! Thirteen killed!"

Jimmy had interrupted his information to dispose of a paper to a man.

"Jimmy Small," repeated the man. "Where do you live?"

5

"Oh, I've got a swell joint on upper Fifth Avenoo," replied the boy, with a wink, "but it's rented fer de season, an' I ain't livin' in it."

"No, I am serious," said Mr. Crosscrab. "I would really like to know."

"Honest? No kiddin'?" inquired Jimmy.

"No what?"

"No kiddin'. Is it de real goods? Youse ain't tryin' t' run up an alley on me, is yer?"

"I don't exactly understand you, but I am really asking because I am interested in you. I have a brother about your age, and I was wondering how he would make out if he had to sell papers for a living."

"Say, take it from me, mister," spoke Jimmy earnestly. "Don't let him do it. Dere's too many in de business now. Don't let him come t' N'York an' sell papers!"

"Oh, he's not very likely to. But you haven't told me where you live."

"Aw, most anywheres. Wherever I kin. If I'm flush wid de coin I takes a bed at de lodgin'-house. When I'm busted—on me uppers—cleaned out—nuthin' doin'—why, I takes a chance at a bench in de park when it's warm. If de cop don't see youse it's all right. Sometimes I hits up an empty box, an' I've done me turn in a hallway. Under a dock ain't so bad, only dere's too many rats t' suit me."

"You lead quite a varied sort of life, don't you?" inquired Mr. Crosscrab.

"Youse kin search me. I ain't got it," replied Jimmy with more good humor than he had previously shown. The man's talk was a little above him.

"I suppose you know your way around New York pretty well, don't you?" the countryman went on.

"Dat's right. Ye can't lose me."

"Are you here almost every day?"

"When I ain't in Wall Street investin' me millions I am."

"Still inclined to jokes, I see," murmured the man. "Well, I'd like to know more about you. You seem like a bright lad, and I may want to ask you some directions about getting around New York. I may see you to-morrow. Does your father allow you to work all day?"

"I ain't got no fader," said Jimmy. He did not speak sadly. He took it as a matter of course, for he had been so long without either father, mother or other relatives to care for him that parents were only a dim recollection to him. "I ain't got nobody," he went on. "I'm in business fer meself."

"Haven't you a mother or a sister or a brother?" asked Mr. Crosscrab, feeling a strong sympathy for the boy.

"Nixy. Not a one."

"How long have you been selling papers?"

"About two years. But say, mister, I don't want to be short wid youse, only I've got t' go an' git some more papes. I'm sold out, an' dis is me busy time. Stop around t'-morrer an' I'll tell ye all I know about N'York."

6

"That's all right," said Mr. Crosscrab, understanding the situation. "I didn't mean to keep you from your work. If I pass this way to-morrow I shall look for you. Here is something to pay you for your trouble."

He held out a coin to Jimmy, who promptly took it. It was a silver quarter.

"Crimps!" exclaimed Jimmy as he saw the money. "Say, youse is all right, that's what youse is! Ye kin ast me questions all day at dat rate."

Mr. Crosscrab, with a smile and a wave of his hand for good-by, passed on toward the Brooklyn Bridge, while Jimmy, hardly able to believe his good fortune, hurried after some more papers.

"I certainly am in luck t'-day," he murmured. "I wonder what ails dat guy? Maybe he's crazy an' believes in givin' all his money away. I wish he'd come by t'-morrer. Crimps! But dis is fine! I'll go see a show t'-night sure!"

CHAPTER II

JIMMY IS OUT OF LUCK

Jimmy bought another supply of papers and hurried back to his corner. But no sooner had he come in sight of it than he saw it was occupied by a large newsboy. The newcomer was a lad much bigger and stronger than our young hero, but in spite of that Jimmy was not going to be deprived of his place without a protest.

"Hey, Bulldog!" he exclaimed, giving the other newsboy the nickname by which he was known, "what ye doin' on my corner?"

"Your corner?" inquired the other, with an ugly grin on his big face, thereby showing two sharp teeth which gave him his name.

"Yep, my corner, Bulldog. I was here all de afternoon sellin' papes an' went t' git some more."

"An' I got it now," added Bulldog Smouder with a leer. "Here ye are, paper! Wuxtry!" he added as a man came up and bought a *World*. It made Jimmy angry to see profits that he thought should be his going into the pockets of his enemy, for Bulldog Smouder was an enemy to all the newsboys excepting those he could not whip. He was a fighter and a bully, and he lost no chance to impose on those weaker or younger than himself. Still, he had no particular grudge against Jimmy, and he would just as quickly have taken the place some other boy regarded as his own as he had preëmpted that recently occupied by our hero.

"Git on off there!" cried Jimmy. "Dat's me place, an' youse knows it."

"I don't know nuttin' but what I sees. I seen this corner an' nobody holdin' it down an' I took it. If youse wants t' keep a good place, what makes youse leave it?"

"I had t' git more papes."

7

"Den youse ought t' have a partner in business wid ye. He could go after papes while youse held de corner. I'll go in whacks wid ye if ye likes. But youse got t' give me half what youse made t'-day."

"I will like pie!"

It had been a good day for Jimmy, and with the quarter Mr. Crosscrab had given him he had more than he had possessed in a long time before. He was not going to divide with Bulldog, even if the latter, from a physical standpoint, was a desirable partner. For Bulldog was lazy. Jimmy knew if there was a union formed he would have to do all the work, while Bulldog would take half the profits and do nothing.

"Ain't ye goin' t' git off me corner?" demanded Jimmy again.

"Naw, I ain't. Now chase yerself. I want t' sell me papes an' go home. Skiddoo fer yours!"

"I'd like t' punch yer face in," muttered Jimmy.

"Try it," advised Bulldog with a grin. "I'll tie youse up in a knot if ye do."

"What's de matter, Bulldog?" asked another newsboy, coming up at that juncture. He had no papers.

"Aw, de kid says I swiped his corner."

"An' so ye did!" cried Jimmy.

"Why didn't ye stay here den?" asked Bulldog.

"I told youse. 'Cause I had 't go after papes."

"Well, youse know what I said. Git a partner."

"Don't youse give him de corner, Bulldog! Youse got as good a right t' it as he has."

"Sure I have, Mike, an' I'm goin' t' stay here, too."

All this time Bulldog was busy selling papers, while the new stock Jimmy had obtained was still undiminished.

"What ye buttin' in fer, Mike Conroy?" asked Jimmy of the newcomer. "It's none of your funeral."

"Aw, g'wan! Guess I kin speak t' Bulldog if I want t'. I'll punch yer nose fer ye if youse gits too fresh."

"I'd like t' see ye do it!" cried Jimmy, but at the same time he took good care not to get too near Mike, who was a worse bully than Bulldog. The latter would not attack smaller boys than himself without some provocation, but Mike Conroy used to beat and kick them every chance he got. He had often hit Jimmy.

"Wuxtry! Wuxtry!" cried Bulldog as the crowd of men hurrying to the ferry came past. He was kept busy selling papers. Poor Jimmy was out of it. His luck had turned, but it was destined to do so even more before the night was over. Still, he had sold a large number of papers. The trouble was he had bought another big supply, and unless he could quickly dispose of them the crowds would soon be gone, and he would have them left on his hands, to return to the offices, thus making no profit.

He sold a few on the outskirts of the throng about Bulldog, but as soon as the latter saw what was going on he made a rush at Jimmy. The latter fled, for he knew that in a fight he was no match for the larger lad.

"Where's your papes?" Bulldog asked Mike during a lull in the business of selling.

"I'm cleaned out. Sold 'em down in Wall Street. Guess I'll take in a theater t'-night. I kin afford it."

"Wish I could. Maybe I'll go wid ye."

"All right. Goin' t' de lodgin'-house?"

"Sure."

"Keep de kid away from here den till I gits sold out an' I'll go wid ye," said Bulldog.

Thus he and Mike formed an alliance against Jimmy. While Bulldog attended to his customers Mike saw to it that Jimmy did not approach the corner; thus the small lad lost what little chance he had of making sales. As he was thinking over the unfairness of it, and wondering where he had better go to dispose of his stock, he was hailed by another lad about his own size.

"Hello, Jim!" cried the newcomer. "What's the matter?"

"Hello, Frank. Aw, Bulldog Smouder run me off me corner. Dat's what he done."

"That's too bad," exclaimed Frank Merton, who, though a newsboy like Jimmy, was better educated. In fact, Frank had not been long in the business. Left an orphan at an early age, an aged aunt had tried to take care of him, but when she was taken ill he found it necessary to go on the streets selling papers, while his aunt was taken to an institution. During the lifetime of his parents he had been sent to school, and so he used better language than did his fellows. He was a bright-faced, pleasant lad, and often did errands, in addition to selling papers, so he could afford to have a regular room at the Newsboys' Lodging House. At night Frank went to evening school.

"Yep, it's tough luck," went on Jimmy. "I went an' bought a new stock, an' I ain't sold five yet."

"I'll help you," generously offered Frank. "I sold out some time ago. That big fire seemed to make every one want a paper. Suppose you give me half your stock, and we'll go over by the bridge entrance and see if we can't sell them. There's a big crowd there yet."

"Dat's a good idea. T'anks. Bulldog was sayin' I ought t' have a partner, an' now I've got one."

"Yes," remarked Frank musingly, "I suppose if two boys did go into partnership they could make more at it than two could working alone. I must think about that."

"Maybe you an' I'll go snooks," proposed Jimmy.

"We'll see," went on Frank. "Anyhow, we'll be partners to-night. Now come on before the crowd gets away."

The two boys hurried back across City Hall Park, and, mingling with the crowd that was hurrying toward Brooklyn, they soon disposed of their papers.

"Here's your money," said Frank, coming up to Jimmy and handing him the change.

"Keep ten cents fer yerself," proposed Jimmy generously, for he was a good-hearted youth in spite of his rather rough ways.

"Oh, no. I made a good profit to-day. I offered to help you, and I didn't expect any pay."

"Ah, g'wan! Take ten cents."

"If you have so much money to give away, why don't you start an account in the Dime Savings Bank?" proposed Frank.

"What's de use?" asked Jimmy. "I'd draw it all out ag'in when I was broke. Youse had better take de ten cents."

"No. I'd rather you'd keep it."

"Den come on an' take in a movin' picture show," proposed Jimmy. "Dere's a dandy on de Bowery. It's a prize-fight, an' ye kin see de knock-out blow as plain as anyt'ing, Sam Schmidt was tellin' me. Come on. I'll pay yer way in. It's only a nickel."

"No. I can't go to-night."

"Why not?"

"I have to go to evening school. The term closes this week."

"Aw, cut it out," advised Jimmy. "Come wid me. We'll have a bully time."

"No, I don't believe I will."

"Den I am. I'm in luck t'-day. Feller give me a quarter fer showin' him where de Brooklyn Bridge was. He was from de country. Guess he was bug-house."

"Bug-house? That's a new one on me."

"Sure, nutty—crazy, ye know, dippy in de lid—off his noodle."

"You certainly have a choice lot of slang," remarked Frank with a smile as he left Jimmy.

"Well, den, I'll have t' go t' de show alone," thought the lad. "Let's see how much I've got."

He counted over his change and found he had more than he expected.

"Dollar an' seventy-seven cents. Crimps! But I'll buy a pack of cigarettes an' have a swell time. Guess I'll git a bit of grub now, an' den I'll be ready fer de show."

"Grub" for Jimmy meant supper. He made a substantial meal on some beans, coffee and bread and what passed for butter in one of the cheapest of the Bowery eating-places. This cost him ten cents. He spent five cents for cigarettes, for Jimmy had learned to smoke them at an early age, and did not consider it wrong, as most of his companions indulged in the same habit.

Puffing on the cigarette, with his hands in his pockets and a comfortable feeling under his belt, Jimmy strolled up the Bowery toward the moving-picture show of the prize-fight. He found a number of persons, including some of his newsboy acquaintances, going in.

"Hello, Bricks," greeted a lad, giving Jimmy the nickname that had been bestowed on him because of his sandy hair.

"Hello yerself, Nosey," replied Jimmy, for the other boy had a very big nose which had earned him this title.

"Goin' in?"

"Sure."

"Take me; I'm broke."

"Come on," invited Jimmy generously, feeling like a small edition of a millionaire. "Have a cigarette?"

"T'anks. Say, youse must be flush wid de coin."

"Oh, I made a little t'-day."

The boys and many grown persons entered the amusement place. They were soon deeply interested in the moving pictures of the prize-fight, yelling and shouting as the photographs of the pugilists were thrown on the white screen.

There were many other moving pictures, the performance lasting over an hour. During a lull, when there was no picture on the screen, Jimmy looked around him. On a seat behind he saw Mike Conroy and Bulldog Smouder, his two enemies of that afternoon.

"Goin' t' punch me after de show?" asked Mike with a leer.

"Aw, cheese it," advised Jimmy. "I'll git square wid youse somehow."

There was no time for further talk, as another picture was shown and the boys were absorbed in that. Jimmy could hear Bulldog and Mike whispering back of him, but he paid no attention to them.

When the show was over and Jimmy was out in the street, Nosey having left him, he began to think of where he should spend the night. This was something he usually left until the last moment.

"Guess I'll treat meself t' a good ten-cent bed t'-night," he said, lighting another cigarette. "What's de use of havin' money if youse can't spend it?"

He put his hand in the pocket where he kept his change. To his surprise his fingers met with no jingling coins.

"Dat's queer," he remarked. "Where's me dough?"

He felt in another pocket. Then in all of them in turn.

"Stung!" he exclaimed. "Some guy has pinched all me coin an' I'm dead broke. I had a dollar an' fifty-two cents left an' now I ain't got a red. Me luck certainly has shook me. What's t' be done?"

CHAPTER III

A BOX FOR A BED

For some time Jimmy stood still in the street. The brilliantly-lighted Bowery stretched away in either direction; a throng of persons, mostly bent on such pleasure as the place afforded, were traveling up and down. No one paid any attention to the friendless newsboy.

"Well, dis is certainly tough luck!" exclaimed Jimmy. "An hour ago I had enough t' live on fer a week, an' now I ain't got enough t' git a cup of coffee. I'm hungry, too, an' I was goin' t' have a feed after de show. I wonder what happened t' me money, anyway?"

Once more he went carefully through his pockets. Some had holes in them, but the one where he had put the change was untorn.

"It couldn't 'a' fell out," mused Jimmy. "Dere ain't no hole, an' I didn't stand on me head. Say, I'll bet some one picked me pocket—dat's what dey did!"

Struck with this idea, he paused in his walk downtown, for he had started toward the lower end of the Bowery.

"Dat's it!" he went on. "Some one swiped me coin, an' I bet I know who done it. Dat Mike Conroy was settin' right back of me. I'll bet he reached over in de dark when I was lookin' at dem pictures an' he swiped it. I t'ought I felt some one pluckin' at me coat, but I didn't have no suspicion it was him. Wait till I see him in de mornin'. I'll go fer him!"

Then another thought came to the luckless lad. He knew he could not hope to force Mike into giving up the money even if he had stolen it. Nor would an appeal to a policeman do any good. In the first place, a bluecoat would not pay much attention to the complaint of a newsboy, as the lads were always fighting more or less among themselves. And, again, Jimmy had no proof against Mike.

"Hold on a minute!" exclaimed our hero in his process of thinking out matters. "I had a cent wid a big hole in it. Dat was me lucky pocket piece, and dat's gone, too. Now if I could find out if Mike's got dat, I'd know if he picked me pocket. I wish I was a detective. I'd find out. He's a mean feller, t' take every cent I had. Now what am I goin' t' do fer a place t' sleep? I guess it's de docks or a box fer mine t'-night," he added with a sigh. "Dere ain't no tick at de bunk house, an' dere ain't no use askin' fer it. I've got t' do de best I kin."

It was not the first time Jimmy had been in such a fix. In fact, it was more frequently this way than any other. In the summer time, which is when this story opens, he often slept out in the open air from choice, and because it saved him the money he would have to spend on a bed. But to-night it was quite cool from the effects of a thundershower that day, and Jimmy thought a place in the lodging-house would be very acceptable.

He would not have cared so much, but he had set his mind on getting a ten-cent bed out of the money he had so unexpectedly received that day, and now it was a keen disappointment to him.

Jimmy frequently made quite a little sum by selling papers, particularly when there was a big accident, but he never thought of saving anything against hard luck or the proverbial "rainy day." He spent his money almost as fast as he earned it, and on several occasions, when in the evening he would have enough to get a bed, he would go to some show, buy cigarettes or play pool until he had nothing left, and would be forced to sleep wherever he could find a place.

He was in exactly this situation now, but through no fault of his own. Still the effect was the same.

"It's up t' me t' look fer a bed now, I s'pose," he went on. "If I saw some of de fellers dey might lend me enough t' git a bed—but what's de use? I ain't goin' t' ask 'em an' git de frozen face. Besides, I'll need somethin' t' stake me t' papes in de mornin', an' I can't afford t' borrow any fer a bed. Me credit ain't any too good."

This was a new thought. Jimmy knew he must have some capital to start him in business the next day or he would fare badly indeed. However, this did not worry him, as the newsboys were frequently in the habit of borrowing from each other enough to "stake" them, or enable them to buy a supply of papers from the publication office. But though nearly any newsboy would lend a companion money for this cause, lending it for a bed was another matter.

"I'll find a bunk some place," thought Jimmy as he plodded on. "It ain't so cold, an' it'll be warmer by mornin'. I know what I'll do, I'll go down t' dat alley where all de big empty boxes is. One of dem'll make a fine bed, an' it'll be warm. Crimps! I'm glad dat entered my head. It's almost as good as de bunk house. Well, anyway, I had a swell time, an' I kin go widout eatin' till I make somethin' in de mornin'. But it's tough luck; it sure is tough luck."

Having thus made the best of his ill-fortune, Jimmy started off toward the alley of which he had spoken. It was in the factory district, on what is known as the "East Side," among the tenements of New York, where the poor lived. Jimmy knew his way about the big city, and he was soon at the place.

It was an alley at the side of a big clothing factory, and piled up in it along the driveway were tiers of big packing boxes from which the contents had been taken and stored in the factory.

Jimmy first took a careful survey of the street before entering the alley, for he had two enemies for whom he must look out—the policeman on the beat and the night watchman of the factory. Both of these individuals objected to boys staying in the packing boxes, and Jimmy more than once had been detected and driven out just as he was ready to go to sleep.

But to-night neither the policeman nor the watchman was in sight. Still Jimmy proceeded cautiously. With a cat-like tread he entered the alley, peering about for a possible sight of the watchman.

"Guess he's inside," thought the boy. "Now if I kin find de box wid de old sacks in it I'll be all to de merry."

The box he referred to was one he had slept in on several other occasions when his funds were gone. He had discovered some old bags, and had piled them up in the packing case, making a rude bed. This box was near an angle of the alley, and the open side of it was up against the building, so that by moving it out a short distance, just wide enough to allow himself to crawl in, Jimmy would have quite a sheltered place.

13

He stole along, pausing every now and then in the dark alley to discover if the watchman was anywhere about. But all was still save for the whistles of the boats on the East River, for the factory ran down to the edge of the docks on the water front.

"All serene, I t'ink," mused the boy. "Now fer a good snooze."

He found the box he was looking for, and to his delight the pile of bags was not disturbed. Jimmy crawled in, shook up the "bed-clothes," stretched out on them and was soon sound asleep, all his troubles for the time being forgotten.

CHAPTER IV

THE NEW BOY

Several hours later, just when it was getting daylight, Jimmy was awakened by hearing a strange noise close to his ear. At first he thought he was dreaming, but when the noise continued—a noise of some one groaning as if in pain—the newsboy sat suddenly up on the pile of bags and looked about him.

A little light came in between the packing box and the side of the factory, and by it Jimmy was startled to perceive that his lodging place had another occupant than himself.

"Hello! Who are youse?" asked Jimmy.

There was no answer save a cry of pain.

"What's de matter?" asked Jimmy again, putting out his hand, for he could not exactly tell whether the dark object was a human being or a big black dog.

"Oh! Oh!" murmured a voice. "My head! My head!"

"Why, it's a kid!" exclaimed Jimmy. "A kid! He must be down on his luck, too, an' crawled in here to bunk. Hey, kid," he went on, "what's de matter wid yer head?"

The new boy gave no answer. Jimmy turned back one of the bags which the stranger had partly pulled up over his shoulders. As he did so a glint of the rising sun struck in between the wall and the edge of the box, lighting up the interior more plainly.

"Why, it's a swell guy!" said Jimmy, as he saw that the boy was very well dressed. "He's got nobby clothes on. I wonder what he's doin' here? Maybe he's run away after readin' dem five-cent weeklies. Crimps! But dis is a go!"

He could now see the stranger distinctly. He was a boy about Jimmy's age, but his clothes were much different from the ragged garments of the newsboy.

"Hey, what's de matter wid youse?" inquired Jimmy, as he saw that the other made no attempt to get up.

"My head! Oh, how it hurts!" murmured the boy. His eyes were closed, and his face was very pale.

14

Jimmy looked more closely at him. Then, to his surprise, he saw there was quite a cut on the boy's forehead. The blood had dried on it, leaving a red streak on the white skin.

"Crimps! Some bloke swiped him one on de noddle!" cried Jimmy. "A nasty one, fer a fact. He's half dead from it. Wonder how in de woild he ever come here? Maybe dey robbed him an' chucked him in here so de cops wouldn't git on to it. I've got t' do somethin'. Hey, kid," he went on, "can't youse git up?"

The boy murmured something Jimmy could not understand.

"Mebby I'd better tell some one," thought the newsboy. "He might die in here. Den if I do dey may say I done it an' I'll git inter trouble. Crimps! But dis is a queer go!"

Kneeling there in the big packing box beside the injured boy Jimmy rapidly thought over the situation. He was considering, in his own way, what was the best thing to do. Finally he decided.

"I'll doctor him a bit meself first," he murmured. "Dat cut needs washin'. Den mebby he'll rouse up a bit. It's early, an' I guess I can sneak out in de yard an' git some water from de faucet. Dat watchman will be tendin' to de fires now."

Peering cautiously out of the box, Jimmy saw no one in the factory yard. He knew where there was a faucet, near a trough where the horses were watered, and usually there was a pail beside it. He had often made his morning toilet there.

Running to it, he drew some water in the pail, and returning to the box, he shoved the receptacle from the wall and used his hand to wash the blood off the other boy's head as he knelt beside him. At the first touch of the cold water the stranger sat up. His eyes opened in a wondering stare, and he exclaimed:

"Where am I?"

15

"Where am I?" asked the strange boy   Page 30

"Where am I?" asked the strange boy. Page *30*

"Now take it easy, kid," advised Jimmy. "Ye're all right, an' ye're in a safe place—anyway, fer a while yet. Here, take a drink of dis; it'll do youse good."

Hardly realizing what he did, the boy drank from the big pail which Jimmy held up for him. This made the stranger feel much better.

"Where am I?" he repeated. "How did I come here?" and he looked about him in surprise as his eyes took in the narrow quarters of the box.

"Youse kin search me, kid," replied Jimmy frankly. "I come in here t' bunk 'cause some bloke swiped all me chink. When I wakes up I sees youse. First I t'ought youse was a dog, den I heard youse moanin' an' I sees de cut on yer head."

"Oh, my head! It hurts very much'"

"Put some more cold water on it," advised the amateur doctor, and the boy did so.

"How's dat?" asked Jimmy.

"Better. I feel much better. But I can't understand how I came here."

"I can't needer. What's yer name?"

"Name?" repeated the other with a wondering stare.

"Sure. What do de odder kids call youse?"

"Oh! My name is Dick."

"Dick? Dick what? Youse must have two names, same's I have."

"Why, yes, of course I have. My name is Dick—Dick—er—I—I—why!" the new boy exclaimed, trying to get up on his knees, but finding he was too weak. "I—I can't remember what my other name is—it's gone from me—something seems to have happened. I remember my first name is Dick, but I can't think what my last name is. Can't you help me?" and he turned a piteous look on Jimmy.

"Dat's queer!" exclaimed Jimmy. "He's forgot his name! What am I up against?"

"Don't you remember my other name?" begged the boy.

"Me? No. How kin I remember it when I never seen youse before? Don't youse know yer own name?"

"I did, but it's gone from me. All I can remember is that they called me Dick."

"Yes, Dick; but Dick what?"

"I don't know." The sufferer tried hard to think what his other name was, but it was impossible to recollect.

"Can't ye remember anythin' else?" asked Jimmy. "Where'd youse come from?"

"I can't remember that, either. All I know is that I got hit on the head. Then it was all dark, and the next thing I recollect I saw you putting water on my head."

"Dis sure is a queer go," murmured Jimmy. "Here I am wid a kid dat can't even remember his own name, an' me dead broke. Oh, yes, dis is a nice state of affairs!"

CHAPTER V

DICK'S NEW NAME

For a minute or more Jimmy thought over the situation. He had been in many strange plights, even in his short life, but never had he known such a situation as this was. He hardly knew what to do.

"Where are we?" asked Dick, while he continued to bathe his head with the water.

"We're in a big box, in a factory alley, down by de East River," replied the newsboy. "Dis is me headquarters when I ain't got no coin."

"I think—I'm not sure—but maybe I have a little money," said Dick. "I remember having some. This place is so cramped I can't get my hand in my pocket."

"Lay down an' stretch out on yer back; den ye kin," advised Jimmy. "Dat's what I have t' do. Dis place ain't hardly big enough fer two."

The other lad did so, and when he put his hand in his pocket the musical jingle of change rewarded him.

"Dat's chink, sure enough!" decided the newsboy. "Now how much is it?"

Dick pulled out a handful of coins. With practiced fingers Jimmy counted the money.

"Two dollars an' fourteen cents," he announced. "Dat ain't so bad. Where'd ye git it? What d'ye work at?"

"I don't know. I can't seem to remember. I can't remember anything but that they called me Dick."

"Dat's queer. But we kin fix dat part of it."

"What part?"

"About de name."

"How do you mean? Do you know my other name?"

"No, but youse got t' have one. Everybody has t' have two names. I'll tell youse what I'll do. I'll give youse another name, an' youse kin keep it till youse gits yer own back."

The other boy looked a little doubtful of this proceeding.

"What will you name me?" he asked.

"I'll call youse Dick Box."

"Dick Box? That's a queer name."

"Well, dis is a queer go all around. Youse says yer first name is Dick. Well, I finds youse in a box, so I'll call youse Dick Box. See?"

"I suppose that will do as well as any other name for the present," agreed Dick, "Perhaps I can remember my other name when my head stops hurting."

"Does it hurt yet?"

"Quite a bit."

"Den let's git outer here," proposed Jimmy. "De watchman'll be along in a little while, and he'll kick us out anyhow. I kin take youse t' a hospital, if youse want's t' go. It don't cost nuttin'. I was dere once, when a cab-horse stepped on me foot. Dey treated me out of sight."

"Oh, I don't think my head is bad enough to go to a hospital for," said Dick. "Perhaps, when I get out in the air, it will feel better. It aches now, and I believe I'm hungry."

"Don't say a word. I am too," replied Jimmy. "But I ain't got de price. Here, better take yer chink, before it gits lost," and he handed Dick back the coins.

"Perhaps you'll—I mean—wouldn't you like to go with me and have some breakfast?" proposed Dick. "I'm a stranger here. By the way, what city am I in?"

"Say, does youse mean dat?"

"Mean what?"

"Don't youse know ye're in N'York?"

"New York? Is this New York? No, I had no idea where I was."

"Well, if dis ain't de limit!" exclaimed Jimmy. "It's gittin' wuss instead of better, Dick Box."

"What is?"

"Dis mystery about youse. Say, honest, youse ain't kiddin' me, is ye?"

"Kidding you? You mean fooling you? Of course not! All I know is that I started away from some place—I can't just remember where—and the next thing I knew I was in the box."

"Well, I guess it's straight goods," admitted Jimmy, with a sigh, "but it sure is a queer go. Youse must have come from some swell joint, den."

"What makes you think so?"

"Why, yer clothes is all to de good. Ye're right in de latest style. Didn't nobody kidnap youse, did dey?"

"Not that I know of."

Dick passed his hand over his head with a bewildered air. It was close in the box, and, now that the sun was up, was getting quite warm.

"Come on; let's git outer here, an' den we kin talk better," proposed the newsboy. He peered out, and, seeing that the coast was clear, he crawled out of the box, followed by Dick.

"I guess we kin take a little scrub in me bathroom, an' den we'll git somethin' t' eat," proposed the street lad, as he led the way to the faucet over the horse-trough. Fortunately the watchman was inside the factory turning on the fires ready for the men who would soon arrive.

Jimmy gave himself a vigorous wash, and then said to Dick:

"Now it's your turn."

Dick appeared to hesitate.

"What's de matter?" asked Jimmy. "It ain't very cold. De cook fergot t' make de fire in de range last night, an' dere ain't no hot water. I'll bounce her if she does it ag'in."

"Why, there isn't any—any towel," said Dick.

"Towel? Well, I guess nixy. Pocket hankcheff's good 'nuff fer me. If ye ain't got none ye kin take mine. It's pretty clean."

"No, thank you, I have a handkerchief."

In spite of the fact that Dick had evidently been used to certain luxuries, he made the best of the improvised bathroom. He washed his face and hands, drying them on a handkerchief of fine quality, at the sight of which Jimmy's eyes opened wider than ever.

"He sure is some rich guy," he said to himself. "Dere's somethin' queer about dis. But I'll git t' de bottom of it, er me name ain't Jimmy Small."

"Where's yer hat?" asked Jimmy of Dick when the washing operations were over.

"That's so. I must have had one."

"Maybe it's back in de box. I'll go look."

He came back in a few seconds with a soft hat and placed it on Dick's head. As he did so he uttered a cry of astonishment.

"What's the matter?" asked Dick.

"Say, no wonder yer mind went back on youse. Dere's a lump as big as a baseball on de back of yer cocoanut. Dat's what made youse fergit yer name, I guess."

Dick felt of the back of his head. Sure enough there was a large swelling there, and it was very painful.

"Who done it?" asked Jimmy.

"I can't remember."

"Dat's funny. If some bloke fetched me a swipe like dat you bet I'd remember it. But come on, we'd better be makin' tracks outer her, 'fore de watchman spots us. I don't want him t' disturb me bed. I might need it ag'in."

"Suppose we go and get some breakfast?" proposed Dick.

"I'm broke, I told youse."

"But I have money enough for both of us."

"Goin' t' stand treat?"

"Why not? It would be a small return for what you did for me."

"Aw, dat's nuttin'. Well, den, come on. I knows a good joint where it's cheap. Have a cigarette?"

It was all the newsboy had to offer, and he meant it well, as he held out the box to Dick.

"No, thank you," replied the other lad. "I don't smoke."

"I'll learn ye," proposed Jimmy generously, "It's easy, an' it's lots of sport."

"I don't think I care for it."

"I didn't needer, first. Made me sick. But I got used to it. Well, I'll light up."

"Before breakfast?"

"Sure. Den I won't be so hungry."

"Oh, don't be afraid of your appetite. I guess I have enough for breakfast for the both of us."

"Dat's all right," Jimmy assured him, "but if dat's all ye got, ye can't live long on it. What youse goin' t' do when dat's gone?"

"That's so; I hadn't thought of it. I wonder what I am going to do? It's queer, but I can't seem to remember anything."

"I guess it is queer. But say, don't worry. I'll look after youse until yer memory comes back."

"Suppose it never comes back?"

Dick looked worried. He was trying to recall something about himself, but it was hard work. Try as he did to think, he could recollect nothing but that his name was Dick.

"Well, no use lookin' fer trouble," remarked Jimmy. "Let's go eat, an' den we'll see what's best t' be done."

The two boys, so strangely contrasted, one evidently from a rich home, to judge by his clothes and manner, the other a gamin of the streets, passed out of the factory yard. As they went the watchman saw them.

"Here!" he called. "Where you fellows going?"

"We're goin' out," replied Jimmy. "Why, did youse want us?"

"You young rascals! You'd better go!" cried the man, shaking his first at them. "If I catch you trying to sneak in here again after wood, I'll set the police after you."

"He don't know we've been in dere all night," said Jimmy with a chuckle to his companion. "Oh, I fooled him all right."

Jimmy led the way to a cheap restaurant he knew of, and though Dick shrank back a little, at the sight of the not very clean place, he went in, for he was very hungry. The two boys made a substantial meal, and Dick paid for it.

"How do you feel now?" asked Jimmy.

"A little better, but I'm rather weak; as if I'd been sick for quite a while."

"Youse don't look very well. What youse needs is a place where ye kin lay down. I know what t' do. Come along."

"Where?"

"To de lodgin'-house. I knows a feller what's got a room dere, an' maybe he'll let ye stay in it t'-day when he's out sellin' papes."

"What do you do for a living, Jimmy?"

"Me? Oh, I sell papes, too, when I got de chink t' buy 'em. I've got t' git a stake dis mornin' an' start in. But I'll take youse t' dat room first. Come on."

Dick, walking with rather trembling footsteps, followed Jimmy, who led the way to the Newsboys' Lodging House. He hoped he would be in time to find Frank Merton, for he had decided to appeal to him to take Dick Box in for a few days.

21

CHAPTER VI

JIMMY ACTS AS NURSE

Frank Merton was just coming down the steps of the Newsboys' Lodging House as Jimmy and Dick reached it.

"Hello, Jimmy," greeted Frank.

"Hello," was the answer. "Where youse goin'?"

"To work. I've got a job doing some gardening for a man over in Brooklyn."

"Dat's a good ways off."

"Yes, but it will pay me better than selling papers. He is one of my regular customers, and when he asked me if I knew any one who would do some work around the garden I offered myself. But why aren't you out with your papers, Jimmy?"

"No chink."

"I'll lend you some money."

"Never mind, Frank. I kin get staked easy enough. I'm goin' t' ask annudder favor of youse."

"What is it?"

"Here's a friend of mine, Dick Box, an' he ain't got no place t' stay. He's sick."

"Dick Box? That's a queer name."

"I give him de last name. Found him in me box," and Jimmy told the circumstances of discovering Dick. During this conversation Dick, who was growing quite pale, sat down on the steps of the building.

"What do you want me to do, Jimmy?" asked Frank.

"I t'ought mebby ye'd let him stay in yer room wid youse fer a day or so, till he's strong. Dat blow he got on his cocoanut sort of knocked him out."

"Of course I will. You came at just a lucky time."

"How's dat?"

"Why, I'm going to stay over in Brooklyn for several days. The gentleman I am to work for is going to allow me to sleep in a spare room while I am weeding and fixing up his garden. I will not need my room, and you and Dick can use it just as well as not."

"Say, dat's de stuff!" exclaimed Jimmy. "Dat's all to de merry. Kin he go right up?"

"Yes, here is my key, and I'll explain to Mr. Snowden, the manager. You had better stay with Dick, Jimmy. He doesn't look well."

"I guess he ain't. I'll look out fer him. Say, Frank, ye're a good feller. I'll pay youse back some day."

"I'm not doing this for pay, Jimmy. Perhaps I will be in trouble myself, some time, and I will want help."

"Well, if youse does, jest call on yours truly," said Jimmy earnestly.

22

Matters were soon explained to the manager, who agreed to let Jimmy and Dick stay in Frank's room during the time he was away. At first Dick insisted on using what little money he had to hire a place, but Jimmy pointed out that, as a strange lad in a big city and sick as he was, he would need all the change he had.

"All right," agreed Dick wearily, for his head was aching greatly.

Frank and Jimmy put him in bed, after he had undressed, and then Frank had to go.

"Perhaps I'd better leave you some money," proposed Frank to Jimmy. "You might have to call a doctor."

"Say, youse must be rich," spoke Jimmy.

"No, but I have a few dollars saved up. You are welcome to some if you need it for Dick."

"Oh, I kin earn plenty, if I once git staked t' some coin fer papes," announced the young newsboy.

"Then let me stake you."

"I have some money left," murmured Dick. "Take that, Jimmy, and buy your papers. I'll not need it."

"Youse can't tell about dat. But I kin double it in a little while, if business is good."

"You had better let me loan you some," proposed Frank.

"No. I'll take his," decided Jimmy. "If he hasn't any room rent t' pay he'll not need any chink right away, an' I'll have some by t'-night. Much obliged, Frank."

"You had better stay here with him to-night," suggested Frank. "The room is big enough for two, and you are welcome to use it."

"T'anks. Mebby I will. But ye'd better skip over t' Brooklyn now, or youse might lose yer job."

"That's so. Do you think he'll be all right?"

"I guess so. He looks pretty sick, though."

"Oh, I'll be all right in a little while," murmured Dick, but the sight of his pale face, with the long red cut on the forehead, did not seem to bear out his words.

However, as Frank could do no particular good, and as he knew he was needed in Brooklyn, he left, bidding the two boys good-by.

"You needn't stay, Jimmy," said Dick. "Take my money, go out, and buy some papers."

"All right. I'm only jest borrowin' it, ye know. I'll pay youse back t'-night."

"That's all right."

Dick spoke in a very faint voice. His face became paler than ever, and his breathing was so strange that Jimmy became alarmed.

"Maybe he's dyin'," he thought. "Guess I'll tell de manager."

The head of the lodging-house came in response to the summons of the newsboy and looked at Dick.

"He ought to have a doctor," Mr. Snowden said. "I'll call in the district doctor."

23

This was a physician, paid by the city, to look after the poor, and he soon came in and examined Dick.

"The boy is suffering from shock," he said. "He needs rest and quiet, and some simple medicine. He'll be all right in a day or so."

"Will his memory come back?" asked Jimmy.

"I think so—yes. It is only gone temporarily."

He left some medicine for Dick, after giving him the first dose.

"Now I am up against it," remarked Jimmy to the manager, as the physician went away.

"What's the matter?"

"Why, I've got t' stay an' take care of him, an' I don't see how I'm goin' t' sell me papes."

"Oh, that's it, eh? Well, don't let that worry you. I think he'll be all right for a while, and I'll look in every hour or so. You go ahead and sell your papers."

The manager was a kind-hearted man and did all he could to help the boys.

"Dat'll be de stuff!" exclaimed Jimmy. "I'll hustle out, an' git t' work. I'll be nurse t' him t'-night. He's a queer kid, an' I'd like t' find out who he is an' where he come from."

"Probably you will, when he gets better," said the manager. "But you'd better hurry out now, if you expect to sell any extras to-day."

Taking a dollar of Dick's money to buy papers with, Jimmy started off. It was a good day for news, there being a number of sensational happenings and every one seemed to want to read about them. Jimmy sold more papers than he had disposed of before in a long time.

"Guess Dick Box must have brought me luck back t' me," he thought. "All de same, I'd like t' git hold of Mike Conroy an' see if he robbed me."

But the bully kept out of Jimmy's way, or else the latter did not see the youth whom he suspected of picking his pocket.

At noon time, having made a dollar and seven cents profit, Jimmy got some dinner and then hurried to the lodging-house to inquire about Dick, as, already, he felt a strong liking for the boy whom he had befriended.

"He's sleeping quietly," said the manager. "I think he is better. Don't worry about him. I'll look after him the rest of the day and you can take charge at night."

The afternoon was always a good time for Jimmy, as the extras were out then and were in great demand. He took his place at his old corner, determined not to leave it, to give Bulldog or any other of the boys a chance to take it away from him. He made arrangements with a bootblack to go after another supply of papers for him, when he sold out, and thus was able to maintain his place.

Toward the close of the day Bulldog appeared with a big bundle of papers under his arm. He intended to establish himself at Broadway and Barclay Street, but, fortunately, a policeman happened to be standing there when he came up and he dared not drive Jimmy away with the officer looking on.

"Dis is de time I fooled youse!" exclaimed Jimmy, as he shook his fist at Bulldog, behind the policeman's back. "Youse dasn't bodder me now."

"Wait till I catch ye!" threatened Bulldog, as then he moved on up Broadway, calling:

"Wuxtry! Wuxtry!"

Jimmy was soon sold out, and, having made nearly two dollars that day, something very unusual for him, but due to the extraordinary demand for papers, he returned to the lodging-house.

"Well, how is he?" he asked the manager.

"A little better, I think. I was up a while ago and he was asking for you."

"Here's where I play bein' nurse," announced Jimmy with a smile.

He found Dick awake and feeling much better. His head no longer ached.

"Kin youse remember who ye be now?" asked Jimmy.

"Not in the least," replied Dick with a sad smile. "It is as much a mystery as ever."

CHAPTER VII

JIMMY CONSIDERS MATTERS

Jimmy was quite disappointed. He had expected that, when Dick felt better, his memory would return, so that the boy could tell something about himself. Now, evidently, this was not to be.

"How did you make out to-day?" asked the lad in bed.

"Fine! Crimps! But everybody on de street seemed t' want a paper. Have a cigarette? I bought a new pack. Blowed meself on account of me good luck."

"No, I don't smoke. I shouldn't think you would."

"Why not? All de fellers does. It's sporty. Say, here's yer dollar back."

"Don't you need it?"

"Naw. I got plenty now. I'll make more t'-morrow."

"Then keep it to pay for what you have done for me."

"Not much! What d' youse t'ink I am? I'm a friend of yourn, an' I'm takin' care of ye; see?

"Yes, but it costs money."

"Well, when I ain't got none I'll borrow some from youse. Now it's time fer yer medicine."

Dick took it, and soon afterward fell into a heavy doze. Jimmy went out, got some supper, and, returning, stretched out on the floor and was soon asleep.

Dick did not awaken until morning, and, when he saw the lad on the floor, he gave such an exclamation of surprise that Jimmy awoke.

25

"What's de matter?" he asked. "Feel worse?"

"No. But the idea of you sleeping on the floor, and me taking up the whole bed! It isn't right. Why didn't you wake me up and make me shove over?"

"Aw, I like sleepin' on de floor. It's like bein' in a hotel, after a night in me box. I'm all right. Feel hungry?"

"A little. I am much better than I was."

"T'ink of yer name yet?"

"No," and Dick shook his head, smiling a little sadly. "I can't seem to remember anything," he went on. "Perhaps, when this lump on my head goes down more, I can do better."

"Well, never mind," answered Jimmy cheerfully. "Youse kin have all de time youse wants."

"I wish I could get up, and help you," proposed Dick. "I think I am well enough."

"No, ye don't!" exclaimed Jimmy. "If youse gits up now youse'll have a perhaps, an' den where'll ye be?"

"A 'perhaps'?" repeated Dick, with a puzzled air.

"Yep. What sick folks gits when dey gits up too quick."

"Oh, you mean a relapse."

"Yep. Dat's it. It's de same t'ing. Now de t'ing fer youse t' do is t' lay quiet. I kin make enough money fer both of us, fer a while yet."

"But I want to help."

"Well, maybe when youse gits well I'll take ye in partnership," proposed Jimmy, with an air as if he was a millionaire.

"Will you, really?"

"Mebby. Now don't git all excited. I'll go out an' bring in some breakfust. What'll ye have?"

"I don't feel very hungry. If I could have an orange, and a cup of coffee, I think it would be enough."

"Crimps! Dat's a light meal," said Jimmy. "I'd starve on dat. Beans is de stuff. Dey're terrible fillin'. Most generally I eats beans. Dey's cheap, too."

"I don't think I care for any this morning."

"All right; I'll tell me cook t' prepare youse somethin' light," and Jimmy, with a bright smile at his joke, left the room, having made a hasty toilet, washing at the basin in the room.

He soon returned with an orange cut up, some toast, and a cup of coffee, which he had bought in a near-by restaurant, where he had his own meal. Dick said the things tasted good, and he certainly looked better after the meal.

"Will youse be all right if I goes out t' business?" asked Jimmy, when Dick had finished. "Me private secretary is sick t'-day," he added, "an' I've got t' work meself."

"Don't worry about me," answered Dick. "I can get along well enough. I am feeling better all the while."

"All right," announced Jimmy. "I'll see ye dis noon."

Once more the plucky little newsboy started out. Business was not so good that day, and he only made a dollar and fifteen cents, but that was enough, considering that he had no room rent to pay for the present, and meals, such as he ate, were cheap.

"I wish I'd meet dat feller—let's see—what was his name?" he mused. "Crabtree?—no, dat wasn't it—Cross-patch?—no, dat ain't it needer—Crabapple?—no—Crosscrab?—dat's it. I wish I'd see him. Maybe he'd want some more information, an' he'd pay fer it."

But, though he kept a lookout for the young countryman, Jimmy did not see him as he stood on his favorite corner selling his papers.

He stopped work about six o'clock and went to the lodging-house. He found Dick able to be up and around the room, but a trifle weak on his legs. "I think I'll be able to go out to-morrow," replied the boy, in response to a question from Jimmy as to how he felt.

"Dat's good. De fresh air'll make youse feel better."

Jimmy was puzzled about what to do. He knew Dick must have come from some well-to-do home, and he suspected that he had either been kidnapped or, perhaps, had wandered away and been hurt, thus forgetting where he lived.

"I s'pose I ought t' tell a cop," thought Jimmy to himself that night after Dick was asleep. "Maybe dere's an alarm been sent out fer him an' his folks is lookin' fer him. Dat's what I'll do. I'll tell a cop."

Dick was not quite so strong the next morning as he thought he would be, but, aside from a little uncertain feeling on his legs, he was all right. That is, not considering his memory, which was as much a blank as when he had awakened to find himself in the box.

"Wait till this afternoon, an' I'll go out wid youse," proposed Jimmy. "I'm too busy t' look after ye dis mornin'."

The truth was he did not want Dick to go out and perhaps get lost again before there was a chance to notify the police, which Jimmy had decided to do. If he could keep Dick in that morning, he would find a certain policeman, with whom he had a slight acquaintance, and tell him the facts.

With this in mind Jimmy set out from the lodging-house, having made Dick promise not to go away or try to walk in the streets until after dinner.

Jimmy bought his stock of papers and was selling them on his usual corner, at the same time keeping watch for the policeman whom he knew and to whom he intended to speak. While thus engaged he was approached by Sam Schmidt, a German newsboy, who was on his way to get a new stock of journals, having sold out.

"Hello, Schmidty!" exclaimed Jimmy. "Seen Hennessy dis mornin'?"

Hennessy was the policeman on that beat.

27

"Nope. I ain't seed nottings of him. Vot's der matter? You vos going to have someboddies arrested yet? Hey?"

"No, not dis time, Dutchy. I want t' ask him some questions."

"Vot about? Vos you in droubles alretty yet?"

"Me? Naw. But anodder kid is."

"So? Vot it is?"

Jimmy thought it might be a good plan to get the advice of some one on Dick's case. He had told neither the lodging-house manager nor the physician all the facts in the matter, and all they knew was that Dick was a friend of his who had been hurt and could not remember how it happened. So he explained the situation to Sam Schmidt.

"Now what would youse do, in my place?" asked Jimmy.

"Vell," replied the German slowly, "I dinks I vould do nottings."

"Do nuttin'? Say, what good is dat?"

"Vell, it dis vay," went on Sam. "Dot feller has goot clothes, you say?"

"Sure he has."

"Den his folks is rich. Ain't it?"

"I s'pose so."

"Vell, den, maybe dey'll offer a rewards for him. Eh? If you turns him over to der bolice, der bolice vill git der rewards. Ain't it?"

"Dat's so. I never t'ought of dat."

"Sure," went on Sam. "Now yust you lay low und you sees vot happens alretty yet."

"Dat's a good idea, Sam," agreed Jimmy. "I'll say nuttin' fer a few days. I ain't much stuck on de cops, anyhow. Dey might ask me too many questions. I'll keep mum fer a few days and see what happens. But how will I know if dere's a reward offered?"

"Vhy, it'll be in der babers. Vun't it?"

"Dat's so. But I can't read, Dutchy."

"So? Dot's bad. Den I tell you vot ve do. I'll keep my vedder eyes vide opens und ven I sees der rewards notice I'll tell you. Eh? How's dot?"

"Fine! I'll give you some of the money, Dutchy, if I git any."

"Dot's nice. Vell, I got t' go me after some more babers. I hopes you gits der big rewards. Likely as not he vos a rich feller und his fader'll pay big money t' git him back. Yust you lays low und said nottings."

"I will, Dutchy. Here ye're, sir! Wuxtry! Full account of de big murder! Wuxtry! Wuxtry!" cried the newsboy, as he saw some possible customers approaching.

Thus Jimmy thought matters over and decided to keep silent regarding Dick. He could not foresee the effect of it, nor what a strange result was to come from his finding of the boy in the box.

CHAPTER VIII

DIM RECOLLECTIONS

When Jimmy went to the lodging-house that noon, he found Dick ready to go out.

"Feelin' all right?" asked the newsboy.

"Very fine indeed, thank you. My head doesn't hurt at all and I think a walk would do me good. Can't I go around with you when you sell papers? I'd like to learn part of the business now, for I'll have to do something for a living, and I don't believe I could do much of anything else."

"Does youse really mean dat?" asked Jimmy suddenly, as a new scheme came into his head.

"Surely. Why not?"

"I didn't s'pose a swell-dressed chap like youse would want t' sell papes."

"I'm afraid I'll not be well dressed very long. Sleeping in that box did not improve my clothes, and, as I haven't any more, I'll have to do something to earn money to buy others. No, indeed, I'd be only too glad if I could sell papers as well as you can."

"Oh, dere's lots of fellers what beats me at it, but den dey has regular stands. Dat's de way t' do it. Have a regular stand somewheres an' customers comes t' youse. Dat's de way t' make money."

"Then why don't you do that way?" asked Dick Box.

"I ain't got de cash t' start in. It takes de coin, an' I has t' spend all I makes t' live on. At dat I ain't livin' very swell—sleepin' in a box. Course it's better since Frank let us have dis room, but he'll be back t'-morrow. We'll have t' light out den."

"But you have earned some money in the last few days, haven't you? And with what little I have we can hire a room. The rent is not very high, is it?"

"Nope. Dollar an' a quarter a week fer dis Frank pays. But I didn't s'pose youse 'ud want t' do it."

"Do what?"

"Bunk in wid a chap like me."

"I don't see why not," replied Dick sturdily. "After what you did for me I'm not going to lose sight of you so soon as that. I'll be only too glad to bunk in with you. In fact, you are the only person I know."

"Can't youse t'ink anyt'ing about yerself—what yer name is an' where ye come from?" asked Jimmy eagerly, for he had in mind the possible reward and he wanted to get a clue as to who Dick's folks might be.

"Not a thing," replied the other, shaking his head a little sadly. "I think I had a good home once, for I have a dim recollection of a big house with lots of ground

29

around it. And I remember a man and a woman who were kind to me. But that's all I can remember, try as hard as I can. It seems as if it was many years ago."

Jimmy shook his head in doubt.

"Dem kind of tips ain't goin' t' be any good t' me," he mused. "I'll have t' depend on Dutchy. If he sees anyt'ing in de papes about a reward he'll tell me. Den, maybe I kin take Dick dere an' git money enough t' buy a newspaper stand. Dat sure would be all to de merry."

"But aren't you going out?" asked Dick, after a pause, during which he had racked his brain to try and remember more about himself.

"Sure, if youse wants t'," replied Jimmy. "Come on an' we'll have grub. Den it'll be time fer de afternoon extras. I hope business is better dan it was yist'day."

The two boys ate in a restaurant near the lodging-house. Dick's appetite was good, and though the food was coarse and not served in very nice style, he ate heartily.

"Don't you like pie?" he asked Jimmy, toward the close of the meal.

"Betcherlife I do."

"Why don't you have some, then?"

"Say, if we is goin' t' hire a room, regular, an' pay rent we can't have pie," replied the newsboy, "dat is except when ye makes a lot extra. Pie is too high livin' fer de likes of newsies."

"Well, suppose we have some to-day," proposed Dick. "I will stand treat this time."

"Dat's good," answered Jimmy gratefully. "I kin eat it all right, but I was goin' slow on de coin."

"I guess you will have to teach me how to use money," went on Dick, as the waiter brought two pieces of pie. "I never earned any in my life, that I can remember, though I used to spend considerable. I'll have to learn business ways now."

"Oh, youse'll learn fast enough," said Jimmy. "It ain't hard not t' spend cash when ye ain't got it, an' dat, mostly, is de complaint I suffer from. I seen me doctor about it, but he said I'd have t' have a change of climate. I kin see meself gittin' dat. But come on. De extras is out now."

Dick followed Jimmy to Newspaper Row, where the latter secured a big bundle of papers from one of the many delivery wagons that were backed up to the curb. Then the newsboy started for his regular stand, getting there just a little ahead of Bulldog.

"Dis is de time I fooled yer," said Jimmy in triumph. "Wuxtry! Wuxtry!" he shouted. "Git de latest wuxtry!"

Bulldog moved off with a sullen look, glancing at Dick as he did so.

"Wonder where Bricks picked up dat kid?" he thought.

Meanwhile Dick was watching with interest the manner in which Jimmy disposed of his papers. Business seemed to be good, as there was quite a crowd in the street, and many persons bought the extras.

"Can't I help you?" he asked Jimmy, during a lull in the stream of pedestrians.

"How d'ye mean?"

"Why, sell papers. Can't I take some and go up and down the street? I think I could sell some."

"Sure ye might," replied Jimmy, glad of the offer. "Here, take a bunch. But ye got t' holler loud, or de men won't notice ye. Shout out dat dere's a big fire or some terrible accident."

"Is there? I didn't see anything in the papers about it."

"Course dere ain't, but de men won't know till after dey has paid fer de paper."

"But that's saying what isn't so."

"Aw, what's de odds? We all does it, an' de men knows we does it, so dey ain't fooled."

"I don't like to do that," objected Dick. "I think a better way would be to look over the papers, see what the principal articles are about, and call them out."

"Aw, dat way wouldn't be no good. What de public wants is t' read about a big fire or a murder or a suicide. Dat's what I allers yells out. Anyhow, I can't tell what's in de papes."

"You can't? Why not?"

"'Cause I can't read."

Dick did not pursue his inquiries any further, as he did not want to hurt Jimmy's feelings.

"Well," he said, "give me some papers and I'll do my best to sell them. But," he added, with a smile, "I'm not going to say there's a murder if there isn't."

"Den youse'll not sell any papes."

Dick took an armful of the journals and started down Broadway. He knew a little of the run of the streets in that section, as Jimmy had told him about them, and he knew he would soon be in the financial district, where the brokers and bankers had their offices.

In spite of his recent accident, and his trouble over forgetting who he was, Dick had a good head for business, even though it was the first time he had tried to sell newspapers. He decided to look over the front pages and learn just what were the principal items of news. He had not forgotten how to read and write, though many other things had slipped from his recollection.

He saw there was a long article concerning a big bank failure, and another about an important notice sent out by the United States Treasurer.

"Those ought to interest the bankers and business men more than murders and fires," thought Dick. "I guess I'll call out about those."

He was, naturally, a little bashful about shouting as did the other newsboys, but he made up his mind that, as he was thrown on his own resources by a queer trick of fate, he must do his best to earn a living.

"Here goes," he said, as he approached a group of well-dressed men standing at Broadway and Cortlandt Street.

"Excuse me," he began, in a clear but not very loud voice, as he stood near the men, "but would any of you gentlemen like to buy the latest extra? It has an account of the failure of the Morrisville Trust Company and a decision of the United States Treasurer on gold shipments. Besides, there is all the latest news."

Probably no regular newsboy in all the big city of New York would have thought to try that means of selling papers. All they did was to shout: "Wuxtry! Wuxtry!" or "Fire! Murder! Suicide!"

"Hello! What's this?" exclaimed one of the gentlemen, turning around and beholding Dick. "What sort of a newsboy is this, who doesn't shout his head off at you?"

"What did you say about the Morrisville Trust Company?" asked another gentleman nervously.

"It has failed. Here is a full account of it," and Dick showed the paper with the story on the front page, under a big, black heading.

"Great Scott!" exclaimed the man who had asked the question. "That's bad for me. Here! Give me a paper."

He fairly snatched one from Dick, and tendered him a nickel.

"Give me one, too," requested another of the group. "I want to read about that gold statement."

"I'll have one also," added a third man, and soon every one had purchased a paper.

"Here is your change," said Dick to the one who had given him the five-cent piece.

"Keep it!" exclaimed the man, not lifting his eyes from the sheet.

Jimmy had told Dick that customers were often thus generous, so the new newsboy felt it was all right to keep the four cents. As he walked away he heard one man say to another:

"That's an intelligent way of selling papers. I wonder why most of the boys think they have to yell themselves hoarse about a fire or a murder? This is the most important news of the day, but it's the first time I heard one of the boys mention it."

"You're right," said another. "That lad looks as if he was fitted for something better than selling papers."

Then the men began to read the news, and Dick, glad to hear that his method was thus approved, moved on toward Wall Street. He found many newsboys in that district, but he kept to the plan he had made, and in much less time than he expected he had sold all his papers and started back to Jimmy for more.

"Youse don't mean t' tell me youse is sold out?" exclaimed his friend as Dick approached.

"Yes, and I didn't have to yell 'Fire' or 'Murder' once."

"Well, dat gits me!" murmured Jimmy in great astonishment.

CHAPTER IX

THE NEWSBOY PARTNERS

With Dick's intelligent aid Jimmy sold more papers that afternoon than he had ever before disposed of in a similar time. The two boys, when the hour came to stop, since the crowds were about done hurrying toward the ferries, found that they had quite a goodly sum between them.

"Well, we might as well go git supper an' den we kin take in a movin'-picture show," said Jimmy. "I know where dere's a swell one. Have a cigarette? Dat's so, I forgot youse didn't smoke. Well, I'll light up."

"Are you going back to Frank's room?" asked Dick.

"Sure. Why not? Frank won't be here till t'-morror."

"I was thinking we had enough money now to hire a room of our own. If we pay a week's rent in advance we'll be sure of a place to stay, and I must admit I don't like sleeping in boxes."

"It'll take a lot of money t' pay a week's rent," objected Jimmy. "We kin hire one by de night, jest as well, an' we'll have more money for sport."

"Yes, but if it should rain to-morrow and we couldn't sell many papers, we wouldn't make much money, but if we invest some now, in a room, we'll be sure of having a dry place to stay."

"Well, mebby youse is right. I never hire a room by de week, 'cause I don't often have coin enough, an' when I does, I generally goes t' a show."

"Don't you think it better to get the room?"

"I s'pose so," replied Jimmy a little doubtfully. Dick was beginning to take matters into his own hands and he made some propositions that Jimmy could hardly understand. For Jimmy took but little thought ahead. If he had money enough to live on for one day that satisfied him, and he let to-morrow take care of itself. But he was willing, at least, to try Dick's way.

Accordingly the boys first had supper and then, going to the lodging-house, inquired of the manager about a room.

"You don't mean to say you're going to get a room by the week, do you, Jimmy?" asked Mr. Snowden, for he knew the habits of the newsboy, who often got a bed in the place for a night, but who had never remained for much longer at a time.

"Sure, me an' me partner wants a good room," was Jimmy's answer. "We's got de coin, too, see!" and he rattled the money in his pocket.

"I'm glad you have. I wish you both would stay here with us regularly. I had a letter from Frank to-day. He inquired about you and Dick and said he would not be back until the end of the week, so you may keep his room until then, if you like."

"I think it will be better if we have our own room at once," said Dick.

"I am glad to hear you say that," went on the manager. "There is nothing like being independent in this world, and though you would be welcome in Frank's room, I think you will feel more business-like if you have one of your own. Eh, Jimmy!"

"Oh, I s'pose so. Whatever me partner says, dat goes."

"Have you gone into partnership?" asked Mr. Snowden, with a smile.

"We have been thinking of it," replied Dick. "I sold some papers for Jimmy to-day, and he said I did well."

"Dat's what he done," declared Jimmy admiringly. "An' he wouldn't yell dat dere was a fire ner a murder. I don't see how he done it."

"I told about the financial news," admitted Dick.

"I should think you two would make a good firm," commented Mr. Snowden. "Now, if you like, I will show you some rooms."

There was not much choice, as the apartments had to be very small and plain, since they rented for very small sums to the poor boys. The beds were hardly large enough for two persons.

"We have one larger room with two cots in it," said the manager, "but that rents for a dollar and a half a week; twenty-five cents more than the others. I don't suppose you would care for that."

"I think we would," said Dick quickly. Somehow he liked the idea of a bed by himself, though Jimmy was unusually clean for a newsboy without a home, as he frequently went to the public baths.

"Will that suit you, Jimmy?" asked Mr. Snowden, for he wanted to be certain both boys would be pleased.

"Sure. Whatever me partner says goes," was the answer, given with a wave of his hand, as though he and Dick were millionaires.

Mr. Snowden took them to the room. It was a fairly good one, and had, besides the two beds, or cots, a wash-stand with a bowl and pitcher, two chairs, and a rocker.

"Say, dis is dead swell!" exclaimed Jimmy, taking a seat in the rocker and moving backward and forward. "De Astor House and de Waldorf-Astoria ain't got nuttin' t' beat dis. Dis is all to de merry."

"I'm glad you like it," said Dick. "I think we'll take it, Mr. Snowden. Here is the rent." It was all Dick had left out of the money he had in his pocket when he awoke to find himself in the box.

"Hold on!" exclaimed Jimmy. "We'll go whacks on dis. I'll pay me share."

"If you are going to be partners why don't you put all your money together and let one of you be the treasurer? Then you can keep track of your expenses," suggested the manager.

"Dat's a good idea," declared Jimmy. "Here, Dick, take what I got an' settle de bills. Youse kin be treasurer an' I'll be de general manager. I can't sign any checks, so dat's de best way."

"I'm afraid it will be a good while before I can sign any checks, either," replied Dick. "But, if you wish, I will take charge of the money. That is if you trust me."

34

"Surest t'ing ye know!" exclaimed Jimmy. "Now, dat's settled, I'll send fer me trunks. Most of me wardrobe is at de tailor's gittin' pressed, but I'll tell him t' send it around here."

"All right," said Mr. Snowden with a laugh, as he took the money for the first week's rent from Dick. "I hope you boys will like it here and will be successful. If there is anything I can do to help you be sure to let me know."

"We will," promised Dick.

The two boys looked at each other for several moments when Mr. Snowden had left. It was a new experience for both of them. Dick, of course, could not tell much about himself, but he felt sure he had never lived in such a place as this, though he was far from despising the simple room. As for Jimmy, never had he expected to live in such comparative luxury. He actually had a place he could call "home."

"Were you in earnest when you said we would go in partnership?" asked Dick, after a pause.

"Sure. Why not? Any kid that kin sell papes de way youse kin, not yellin' about a fire or a murder, kin be a partner wid me as long as he likes. I'm willin' if youse is. We've got money now t' take us troo de week an' stack up wid papes every day. Sure, we'll be partners, if youse likes de idea."

"I certainly do, but I can't be sure of selling as many papers every day as I sold to-day. I did better than I thought I would."

"Don't let dat worry youse. Everybody is down on deir luck once in a while. What d'ye say? Is it a go?"

"As far as I'm concerned, yes. I'm much obliged to you for taking me into the firm."

"Oh, dat's all right. Don't mention it. If youse hear of any of dem millionaires in Wall Street wantin' an interest, tell 'em de place is filled."

Thus Jimmy Small and Dick Box (as we must continue to call the strange lad for a time) formed a newsboy partnership that was destined to have a greater influence on their lives than either of them suspected.

CHAPTER X

AN ENCOUNTER WITH CONROY

"Well, now we's settled in our mansion," said Jimmy, "s'pose we takes a night off an' goes t' see a show."

"What kind?"

"Well, we kin git under de roof fer a quarter at a regular theater, or we kin git a seat in de top gallery of a continuous performance fer fifteen coppers. Den dere's de movin'-picture shows dat cost a nickel. I generally takes dem in, 'cause I ain't allers so flush wid de coin as I am now. What d'ye say t' a movin'-picture show?"

"I've no objections. I never saw one. What are they like?"

"Never saw one! Crimps! If I didn't see a show once in a while I'd feel like a dead one!"

"That is, I suppose I never saw one," went on Dick, with a puzzled look. "Of course I can't remember what happened before—before I got to the box," he added with a smile.

"Well, we'll take in a movin'-picture show, an' mebby youse kin remember if youse ever saw one before."

"All right," agreed Dick, and they started out together.

The Bowery was ablaze with lights and there was quite a crowd in the street. It was the first night Dick had been out since his illness, and, before that, he could not remember having seen New York lighted up. He was much interested in everything he saw.

"Wait a minute," exclaimed Jimmy, as they passed a tobacco store. "I've got t' git some cigarettes. I'm all out."

He hurried inside, and came out smoking one, putting the remainder of the box in his pocket.

"I don't see why youse don't take a smoke," he said to Dick.

"I suppose because I never learned how. Do you like it?"

"Do I? Say, it's all to de merry. Better have one."

"No, thank you. I don't think it's a good thing for boys to smoke."

"Why not?"

"I've read somewhere that it makes them stunted. And it isn't good for their brains."

"Huh! It ain't hurt me none."

"How long have you been smoking?"

"Ever since I was twelve, an' I'm goin' on sixteen now. I keep right on growin'. Course I ain't sayin' much of me brain, but den I guess I never had much."

"I think you are very bright and quick," said Dick with earnestness. "If you want to get on in the world I wouldn't think smoking would be good for you."

"Aw, all de kids does it. An' look at de men. Why, I seen a millionaire once an' he was smokin' a big black cigar."

"Perhaps; but I don't believe he smoked when he was a boy."

"Aw, sure he did. Smokin's fun."

"I wish you'd give it up," went on Dick. "It must cost you something."

"Oh, not much. Only a nickel a day. Crimps! I knows some fellers dat smokes three packs a day."

"That is too many, even for a man, I would think. But if you only spent five cents a day, that's thirty-five cents a week."

"All dat?" inquired Jimmy. "I never s'posed it was so high. Maybe I'm spendin' too much."

"Thirty-five cents is nearly a quarter of the amount we pay a week for our room," went on Dick.

"Well, I'll cut down some," promised Jimmy, "but I ain't goin' t' stop altogedder."

Dick wisely forebore to pursue the matter any further. By this time they were at the place where the moving pictures were shown, and Dick, who had most of the money, though Jimmy kept some, bought two tickets.

"Dere's a friend of mine. I want t' speak t' him," said Jimmy as they entered the place, for the performance had not yet begun after the last intermission. The newsboy saw Sam Schmidt in the next aisle.

"Say, Dutchy," he asked in a whisper, "did youse see anyt'ing about dat reward fer me friend yet?"

"No, not yet," replied the German youth. "I keeps lookin' in der baber, but I ain't seed nottings about no rewards fer der poy. Dere is a rewards fer a mans, und vun fer a vomans, but not any for dot poy. But vait, don't give him up t' der bolice yet."

"I ain't goin t'. Him an' me is partners."

"Dot's right. Keep him safe py you, und mebby you'll git moneys for him. I'll keep on der vatch out."

"Dat's right, Dutchy. Say, youse ain't seen nuttin' of Mike Conroy lately, have youse?"

"Sure, I seen him und dot dog feller out in der street a while agos. I dinks dey vos comin's in here."

"What dog feller?"

"Der vun dey calls Bulldogs."

"Oh, him. Well, I've got somethin' t' settle with Mike Conroy. I t'ink he robbed me."

Suddenly the lights were turned off, and the man in charge of the picture machine prepared to operate it. Jimmy made his way back to where Dick sat, his conversation with the German newsboy not having been overheard.

"I hope dey have a prize-fight or a robbery picture," said Jimmy.

"Do you like those best?" asked Dick.

"Bettcherlife! Dem's bully. Dey have one scene where a feller gits a knockout blow right in de middle of de ring, an' youse kin see him fall over, dead to de woild. Den dere's annuder where a feller shoots fifteen Injuns out West."

"I think I'd like something quieter, like scenes of travel in foreign lands."

"Oh, dey uster have dem, but de fellers hissed when dey was showed an' dey took 'em off."

The pictures now began, and Dick was much interested in one showing the fire department in action. It was very realistic, though of course it was all arranged purposely for the picture machines, and the woman jumping from the window of a burning building, though it looked very real and dangerous, was only an imitation. Dick at first did not realize this, but Jimmy, who had acquired a fund of knowledge on these points, enlightened him.

There was some singing by a performer after this picture, and when the lights were turned up Jimmy saw, sitting not far from him, Mike Conroy and his crony, Bulldog.

"Dere he is!" he exclaimed when the singer had finished.

"Who?" asked Dick.

"A feller I t'ink robbed me. I'm goin' t' tackle him after de show."

"Are you going to fight?"

"I will if youse'll stand by me."

"I'm afraid I'm not much of a fighter. I'd rather not."

"Well, mebby it's just as well, 'cause Mike an' Bulldog could lick de both of us. But I'll tell him he robbed me."

During the performance Jimmy smoked several cigarettes, as did nearly every one else in the place, until the room was so thick with the vapor that it was hard to see the pictures clearly, and it was difficult for Dick to breathe.

"Dey didn't have no prize-fight, an' dat robbery picture was rotten," declared Jimmy when the performance was over, and the two boys made their way out. "I ain't comin' here no more."

"I don't believe I will either," declared Dick with a cough.

"Don't youse like it?"

"Oh, yes, some of the pictures were very interesting, but I could hardly breathe on account of the smoke."

"Oh, youse'll git used t' dat," declared Jimmy. "If youse took a cigarette yerself youse wouldn't mind it."

"I'm afraid that wouldn't make much difference. But it's nice out here."

"Wait till I see if I kin spot Mike," proposed Jimmy, and they took their position near the doorway. Soon Bulldog and his crony came out.

"Hey, Conroy," began Jimmy, stepping up to the larger youth. "What'd youse do wid me money?"

"Your money? What's de kid talkin' about?" and Mike turned to Bulldog.

"Search me," was the answer. "Hit him a poke an' come on."

"You hit me an' I'll tell dat cop over dere," threatened Jimmy, motioning toward a bluecoat. "Youse swiped some chink offen me, Mike, an' I want it."

"Aw, fergit it," advised the other. "Who says I took any of your money? You never had any."

"I had more'n a dollar an' a half when I was here t' de show last time, an' youse an' Bulldog sat behind me. When I come out I didn't have a red cent left."

"An' youse t'ink I took it!" exclaimed Mike. "Say, youse has nerve, youse has."

"Gimme de money," demanded Jimmy.

"I'll give ye a poke in de ribs if ye bodders me any more!" cried Conroy, making a dart toward Jimmy as he saw that the policeman was moving away.

"Aw, who's afraid of youse?" asked Jimmy boldly, but he looked to see if a way of retreat was clear. The instant his head was turned Mike made a rush for him and hit Jimmy in the face. Then before the boy could strike back at him Conroy had dodged away and was off down the street, running, while Bulldog Smouder followed. Mike was not going to risk remaining after hitting Jimmy when there was a policeman within call.

"Did he hurt you much?" asked Dick sympathetically.

"Naw," bravely replied Jimmy. "Wait till I git him off alone somewhere an' I'll have a try at lickin' him. I'll practice up an' see if I can't do him."

Then to console his wounded spirit, as well as to forget the pain of the blow, for it had been a hard one, Jimmy lighted another cigarette.

CHAPTER XI

PLANNING A TRICK

While Jimmy and Dick went to their room in the lodging-house, Mike Conroy and Bulldog Smouder, after turning a corner and finding there was no pursuit after them, slackened their pace.

"What'd youse run for?" asked Bulldog. "I'd 'a' helped if it come t' a fight."

"Aw, Bricks can't fight me," replied Mike. "But I didn't want dat cop t' see me. He's been lookin' fer me."

"Fer what?"

"Aw, he t'inks I swiped some fruit offen an Italian's stand, an' de Dago made a complaint ag'inst me."

"Did youse take any?"

"Jest a few bananas. But don't say nuttin'."

"Course not. I didn't squeal when youse took Bricks' coin, did I?"

"Go easy on dat," advised Mike. "Somebody might hear. I give youse half, anyhow."

"I know dat. Dat's why I didn't squeal."

"Say, I wonder who dat well-dressed guy was wid Bricks?" went on Mike. "I seen him t'-day sellin' papes wid him."

"I don't know. Maybe Dutchy does."

"How would he know?"

"I seen Jimmy talkin' t' him kinder serious jest as we come in t'-night."

"Where does Dutchy hang out?"

"Down on Mulberry Street. Why?"

"Let's find him an' see if he knows anyt'ing about de new kid wid Bricks," proposed Bulldog. "Dere's somethin' funny about him. Why, he's a reg'lar swell, an' travelin' wid Jimmy looks queer."

"What do youse t'ink it is?"

"I've got a suspicion he might have runned away from home t' see life in a great city as it's played in de theaters."

"Well, suppose he has?"

"Maybe we kin pipe his folks off as t' where he is an' git a reward."

"Dat's so! Bully fer you, Bulldog. Come on, we'll see if we can spot Dutchy."

The two plotters found the German newsboy after a little search. Bulldog had agreed to do the talking.

"Hello, Dutchy," he greeted. "Say, don't youse want a cigarette?"

"Sure. I ain't had no luck dese days, und I ain't got no money fer smokes."

"Well, here's a couple," went on Bulldog, for he wanted to get on the right side of the other lad.

"Ach! Now I feels petter alretty yet," announced Sam as he lighted the cigarette, for he, like nearly all the other newsboys, was addicted to smoking.

"I saw Jimmy Small an' his new partner t'-night," went on Bulldog. "It's a wonder dat new kid don't go back home."

"Home? Did youse know vere his home vos?" asked the German, thinking from Bulldog's remark that he must know something of Dick.

"Well, maybe I do. What do youse know about him?"

"Vos dere a rewards for him in de baber?" asked Sam in his turn. "I vos lookin' fer it, but I don't see any."

"I don't know; but what did you hear about him? He's got a swell home, I understand, an' his dad wants him t' come back."

"I knowed he vould!" exclaimed Sam. "Tell me, vere is his home? I goes me und dells Jimmy. He is goin' to divide der rewards mit me."

"Where'd he pick up de kid?" asked Bulldog, determined to get all the information he could without disclosing the fact that he knew nothing of Dick.

The German lad, who had been deceived by Bulldog's manner, readily told all he knew of Dick, and how he had been found. Bulldog and his crony exchanged glances.

"Now tells me vere his home is und I tells it t' Jimmy," went on Sam. "We must hurry t' git der rewards pefore der bolice."

"Aw, I don't know anyt'ing about him," replied Bulldog with a laugh. "I was only foolin' youse."

"Foolin'! So? Dot's a yoke, hey? Vell, I'm sorry I told you anydings, und I'll tells Jimmy t' be on der lookouts by you both alretty yet."

"Oh, dat's all right," spoke Bulldog quickly, for he did not want Jimmy to learn he had been making inquiries concerning Dick. "I didn't t'ink you'd mind, Dutchy. Here, have some more cigarettes, an' t'-morrow night we'll take youse t' a show."

"Is dot some more foolin's?" asked the German boy suspiciously.

"Naw, dat's de straight goods; won't we, Mike?"

"Sure."

"Dot's all right, den. I vun't say noddings. But it's queer about dot Dick Box. He has forgotten all about hisself, und he don't even know vot his own name is. Ach! Dot's a yoke, too, I dinks!" and the German boy, laughing himself back into good nature, left the two plotters.

"Well, what next?" asked Mike of his crony, after Sam's departure.

"I don't know exactly. I've got t' t'ink it out. But I'll bet we kin find out where de kid belongs an' git dat reward away from Jimmy. He don't know nuttin'. He can't read or write."

"No, but Dutchy kin, an' maybe he'll help him. Youse heard what he said about lookin' fer a reward in de papers."

"Oh, dat's all right. I'll fix Dutchy. I'll give him a song an' dance, an' he won't know whether he's standin' on his head or his feet. Youse leave Dutchy t' me. I'll 'tend t' him."

"All right. Go ahead; but I git half de reward."

"Sure. Ain't we pals?"

"What ye goin' t' do foist?"

"I'm goin' t' have a talk wid de police."

"Dat'll give de whole t'ing away."

"Naw. Not de way I do it. I knows a detective, an' I kin find out on de quiet if dere's any alarm out fer a boy answerin' Dick's description. Dat's what I'll do foist."

Meanwhile Dick and Jimmy, all unconscious of the plot against them, were in their new room discussing plans for the next day.

CHAPTER XII

DICK BECOMES A TEACHER

For several days Dick and Jimmy did well as partners in the newspaper business. There happened to be considerable news, and there was a good demand for papers. Consequently the boys sold a large number and their earnings were considerable.

"Crimps! But we'll be millionaires if dis keeps on," remarked Jimmy one night, when they were in their room counting up their cash.

"Hardly that," replied Dick, "but we have enough for our next week's room rent, sufficient to live on and three dollars besides. I think we had better open a bank account with that."

"A bank account?"

"Yes; why not? Frank Merton told me about the Dime Savings Bank, where he puts his money."

On Frank's return from Brooklyn he had renewed his acquaintance with Dick, and the two boys had taken quite a liking to one another.

"Well, youse is de treasurer of dis firm," replied Jimmy. "If youse t'inks a bank account is de proper t'ing, why, go ahead an' open it. I guess I kin stand it if youse kin."

"It will be a good thing in case we have bad luck. We'll have something to fall back on for our room rent."

"All right, sport," exclaimed Jimmy, who occasionally did not use Dick's name in speaking to him, calling him whatever he happened to think of in the way of street slang. "Go ahead, cully. I'm game."

So the next day Dick opened a bank account in his name, as Jimmy could not sign the book, a fact of which the newsboy was not at all ashamed. Nor could he read more than the titles of the different papers he carried, and these were distinguished by him more by the different kinds of type than by the difference in letters.

Dick's fear about poor business was justified. A heavy rain storm took place that afternoon, just at the time when the extras came out. It seemed as if every one got in out of the wet, and there were few persons on the street to buy papers. The rain kept up until long after dark, and the two partners, who had to go out rain or shine, found they had not sold ten papers between them.

"Dis is de time we're up ag'inst it," remarked Jimmy rather dismally as they took back to the newspaper offices the unsold copies and started for their room.

"Well, we can't always expect to do as good business as we did at first. Anyhow, we don't have to worry about our room rent nor our supper. To-morrow we'll probably do better."

"Let's take in a show," proposed Jimmy. "I feel sort of low in me mind, an' a good show'll cheer me up."

"Do you think we can afford it? We haven't made our expenses to-day, and I don't believe we should waste any money on a show. We ought to wait until we have had better luck. Of course half the money is yours, and you can do as you please. Only I'm not going to spend any of mine on a show. Besides, we saw one this week."

"Well, maybe I'd better stay home den," agreed Jimmy with a sigh. "Anyhow, I've got some cigarettes an' I'll have a smoke."

"Jimmy," said Dick with a sudden resolve, "I wish you'd do me a favor."

"Sure. What is it?"

"Don't be so quick to promise until you hear what it is. Perhaps you'll not want to do it."

"Why, I'd do anyt'ing fer youse, Dick."

"Will you give up smoking?"

"What's dat?" asked Jimmy suddenly, pausing in the act of lighting his cigarette.

"I wish you would stop smoking. It can't do you any good, and I'm sure it must do you harm."

"Stop smokin'? Say, I—I don't believe I kin. Honest I don't. Seems like whenever I feel bad a cigarette makes me feel fine."

"That's just the trouble. You will get to depend on them to make you feel good, and you'll have to keep on smoking more and more as you grow older."

"Aw, what's de harm? All de kids does it, an' look at de men."

"I know plenty of them do, but I don't believe any of them can say it benefits them. I read in the paper the other day that a doctor said it was very injurious for boys to smoke. I saved the article. You ought to read it."

"Huh! I can't read me own name."

"Oh, excuse me. I didn't mean to make you feel bad," spoke Dick quickly. "I forgot you couldn't read."

"Dat's all right, cully. Me feelin's ain't hurted."

"Would you like to read?" asked Dick as an idea came to him.

"Say, would I? Betcherlife I would. But I don't s'pose I ever kin learn."

"I don't see why not."

"How could I? Who'd teach a newsie like me t' read?"

"I would, Jimmy, if you wanted me to."

"No kiddin'?"

"No 'kidding,' as you call it. I would like to very much."

"Does ye t'ink I kin learn?"

"I don't see why not. You are bright and quick, and you have a good memory, for you know where almost every street in New York is located."

"Oh, dat's easy; but dem letters—every one looks so much alike dat I never kin tell 'em apart."

"Oh, they are all different, as I can soon show you. Will you try?"

"Sure I will. Crimps! But t'ink of me learnin' t' read!"

"And why don't you include writing while you're about it?" asked Dick with a smile.

"Writin'? Say, if I lived t' be a hundred years old I might learn t' scribble me own name, but dat's all."

"Oh, no. I am sure you could learn to read and write. If you like I will teach you both."

"Start in den!" exclaimed Jimmy with the air of a martyr. "De sooner de quicker. Say, tell ye what I'll do," he added as he put back in the box the cigarette he had not lighted. "If youse kin teach me t' read an' write I'll—I'll stop smokin'."

"Really?" asked Dick, much delighted.

"Sure. I guess I kin, but I'd like a cigarette awful jest now. Maybe if I smoke one now I kin quit easier."

43

"If you are going to stop, you might as well stop at once," said Dick firmly, for he wanted to reform his partner if he could.

"All right," agreed Jimmy with a sigh, and he put the box of cigarettes back in his pocket.

"What are you going to do with them?" asked Dick.

"I'll give 'em t' Dutchy. He smokes."

"Throw them away. It isn't good for Sam to smoke, and you shouldn't give him the chance."

This proposition was almost too much for Jimmy, used as he was to the life of the streets, but he had started on a new line of conduct and, at least for a time, he was going to follow it.

He hesitated a moment, and then, with something like a sigh of regret, he went to the window of the room and tossed the box out into the air court. The cigarettes fell to the pavement below, where the rain soon spoiled them.

"Now for the first lesson," said Dick. "We'll begin on the letters," and finding in an old newspaper an advertisement where the print was large, he began to teach Jimmy the rudiments of reading.

"We'll begin on the letters," said Dick   *Page 92*

"We'll begin on the letters," said Dick. Page 92

The newsboy was eager to learn, and as Dick was an enthusiastic teacher, the lesson went on surprisingly well. It was nearly midnight before they stopped, so quickly did the time pass.

"How do you like it?" asked Dick as they got ready for bed.

"It's—it's kinder queer," replied Jimmy. "I can't seem to remember whether de cross piece of de letter T is on de top or on de bottom, an' I've clean forgot which is knocked flat on de side—de D or de O."

"Oh, you'll soon remember all that. Don't be discouraged. It will come in time," said Dick encouragingly; and then the two newsboy partners said good-night and crawled between the blankets.

CHAPTER XIII

BULLDOG QUESTIONS DICK

Business was better for the two boys the next day, as the rain had ceased and there was a lively demand for papers. As soon as the first rush was over Jimmy, who was as usual at his place at Broadway and Barclay Street, turned to an advertisement in one of the papers and began to pick out the letters. He was engaged in this occupation when a man stopped in front of him, but at first Jimmy did not see him.

"Aren't you selling any papers to-day?" asked the man.

"Sure," replied Jimmy, alive in an instant to business. "*Sun, Woild, Herald, Times, Joinal*—why—why——" he exclaimed as he looked up and saw Mr. Crosscrab, the young man from Vermont, standing in front of him.

"I see you remember me," said Mr. Crosscrab, smiling.

"Dat's what I do. Did youse git t' Brooklyn all right?"

"Yes, and when I got there I found my aunt very sick. That is why I haven't been back to New York. This is the first chance I have had to come over, and I took the opportunity of looking for you."

"Well, I'm right on de job. Have a paper?"

"I'll take a *Sun*," and the countryman handed Jimmy a nickel.

"Dat's all right," replied the newsboy in a spirit of generosity. "Have one on me."

"Are you giving papers away?"

"To me friends, yep."

"Well, I don't expect to get my news that way, though I'm glad you consider me a friend. I insist on paying for this."

"But didn't youse give me a quarter?"

"That was for information furnished. I consider I got twenty-five cents' worth from you. Now I want to buy a paper. If you won't sell it, I'll get one from some other boy."

"Well, if youse puts it dat way I'll take de coin," said Jimmy, though he honestly wanted Mr. Crosscrab to take a paper for nothing.

"How have you been since I last saw you?" asked the young man.

"Fine. I've got a partner in me business now."

"Is that so? Who is he?"

"Dick Box."

46

"Dick Box? What a strange name."

"Well, I found him in a queer place—in a box—so I give him dat name. He don't know any udder."

"That's odd. Well, I am going up to Central Park. Which is the best way to get there?"

Jimmy gave the necessary directions.

"I'd like to have you come along," proposed Mr. Crosscrab, who had taken quite a liking to Jimmy.

"Can't leave me business. Me partner'd git mad if I made him do all de work."

"No, probably it wouldn't be right. Well, perhaps I will see him some day and take you both along. I need a guide to show me around New York. I suppose you would come if I made it worth your while?"

"I'll have t' speak t' me partner," replied Jimmy with a laugh.

"Where do you live?"

"Newsboys' Lodgin' House. We've got a regular room, an' we're dead swell. Come an' see us."

"Perhaps I will some time," and with a pleasant smile Mr. Crosscrab bade Jimmy good-by.

"Dick Box," mused the country young man as he walked away. "That is certainly an odd name. I used to know a boy named Dick, but his last name wasn't Box nor anything like it."

During this time Dick was selling papers in the financial district. He found that it was an advantage to follow his method of calling the attention of the bankers and brokers to news in which they were interested rather than to more sensational items.

He sold nearly as many papers as did Jimmy, who had years of experience to his credit. Dick soon became well known as a newsboy in the moneyed section of the city, and many rich men bought their papers regularly from him. His frank and courteous manners, and the quiet, business-like way in which he went about gained him a number of friends.

It also gained him enemies among the other newsboys, who did not like to see their territory invaded by a newcomer, especially one who did so well.

But as the financial district was patroled by several policemen and detectives to prevent robberies, none of the jealous newsboys dared attack Dick and engage him in a fight, which a number of them wanted to do to pay him back for taking some of their trade away.

Dick was doing nothing wrong, and he knew it. The streets were free, and if he could sell papers by his own methods, he knew he was within his rights.

Still there was much feeling against him, and among those who considered him their especial enemy was Bulldog Smouder. He had often sold newspapers in Wall Street, and he noted a falling off in his sales since Dick's advent. Bulldog's method was like that of his companions. He would yell out at the top of his voice, and call some piece of news which might or might not be true. And whatever it was, he mumbled his words so that no one could understand him.

47

Whenever he saw a man put his hand in his pocket he would assume that the man wanted a paper, and he would rush up and thrust one in his face.

On one occasion a gentleman who frequently bought a paper of Dick approached him, putting his hand in his pocket to extract a coin. The motion was observed by Bulldog, who rushed forward with such eagerness that he ran into the man.

"Here! What are you trying to do!" exclaimed the customer.

"Wuxtry! Don't youse want a wuxtry? All de latest news!" exclaimed the big newsboy.

"Certainly I want a paper, but I prefer to buy it of this lad," and he purchased one from Dick.

"I'll fix youse fer dis!" threatened Bulldog when the man had gone. Perhaps he might have undertaken to chastise Dick then and there had it not been for the presence of a big policeman on the next corner.

"What have I done?" asked Dick.

"Youse is takin' all me customers away."

"I didn't do anything to induce that man to buy of me."

"Yes, youse did."

"What did I do?"

"Well, I don't know what it was, but youse has got t' git outer here. Dis is me stampin' ground, an' I want youse t' git."

"Suppose I don't?" asked Dick, who was not afraid, even if Bulldog was the larger.

"Well, you'll see. Who are youse, anyhow? Comin' t' N'York an' buttin' in here where youse ain't wanted. Why don't youse go back home?"

"I would if I knew where my home was," spoke Dick quietly, for he made no secret of his queer plight.

"Say, kid, honest, don't youse remember anyt'ing about yerself?" asked Bulldog with a sudden assumption of friendliness, for he happened to remember the conversation he and Mike Conroy had had concerning Dick, and he thought this a good chance to further the plot which the two had made.

"I can remember very little about what happened before I met Jimmy Small."

"Don't youse know what kind of a place youse lived in?"

"I haven't the least idea."

"An' can't youse remember yer own name?"

"Only the first part of it."

"Well, dat's a queer go! Would youse like t' git back home, kid?"

"Indeed I would. Why, do you know anything about me? My mind seems in a daze whenever I try to think about it. If you know anything, please tell me."

"Naw, I don't know nuttin'. Say, youse didn't run away, did youse? Youse ain't comin' no game like dat, is yer?"

"No, certainly not," replied Dick, his face flushing at the insinuation.

"Well, dat's queer," murmured Bulldog as he turned away. Then he started suddenly as he saw coming toward him a man whom he knew. It was a detective from police headquarters, and Bulldog had frequently given the man information about petty thieves.

"Say," said Bulldog in a low tone to the detective as the latter reached him, "I want t' ask youse a few questions. Come in here," and he motioned to a hallway. The detective, who was inclined to be friendly with the newsboy, thinking he might have some future use for him, complied, and soon the two were in conversation.

CHAPTER XIV

JIMMY'S FURTHER PROGRESS

Meanwhile Dick, all unconscious of the plot being woven about him, continued to sell his papers. When he was out he went to the delivery wagon and got more, and he remained in the financial district until three o'clock, when, as that marks the close of the day's business, there was not much chance to sell any more papers.

Then he went up to report to Jimmy and help him dispose of his stock by circulating around City Hall Park and the streets leading to the ferries.

"Well, dis ain't so bad," remarked Jimmy as they went to supper that evening, calculating on the way how much they had taken in.

"No, indeed," said his partner. "If this keeps on we can soon start a regular stand."

"Crimps! Dat would be fine! But I guess we'll have t' have more money saved up. All de good places is taken, and we'd have t' buy somebody out."

"Oh, yes, we'll have to have more money," agreed Dick. "But if all goes well we can put another dollar in the bank this week."

"Dat's de stuff. Crimps! but I'm hungry! Guess I'll have a——" Jimmy stopped suddenly as he put his hand in his pocket.

"What's the matter? Lost your money?" asked Dick anxiously.

"Nope. I was jest goin'—jest goin' t' smoke a cigarette, but I forgot——"

"I'm glad you remembered in time. Do you find it hard to give them up?"

"It's kinder hard—jest now."

"Then come on, let's hurry up and have supper and you'll not think of smoking."

"All right," Jimmy agreed, but it was quite a struggle for the lad. The cigarette habit had taken more of a hold on him than he supposed, and he felt that he must smoke. But he determined to keep his word, and as he was a boy of some strength of character, in spite of his surroundings, he did not readily give in to the temptation.

After supper the reading lesson was resumed, and Dick also began to instruct his pupil in the mysteries of writing. It was not easy work, but Dick was not discouraged.

Jimmy had one merit, he really wanted to learn; for he was sharp and shrewd, and he saw what an advantage it was to Dick to be able to read and call out intelligently the items of news. In this way Dick could sell as many papers as could Jimmy, and with half the effort, for Jimmy made himself hoarse with his frequent cries of "Wuxtry!" Then, too, Jimmy was aware of how much better off he was since he had formed a partnership with Dick. He actually had money in the bank, a thing he never dreamed of before, and he had a good room, which formerly was such a rare occurrence for him that he could count on the fingers of one hand the number of times it had happened since he had had to shift for himself. So Jimmy determined to do his best to learn to read and write.

In a week the newsboy knew the alphabet, and could spell a few simple words. The writing came slower, but he was making progress.

Then another improvement took place. As he learned to spell the words he also learned how to pronounce them correctly. He saw that "the" spelled a different word from "de," as he was accustomed to pronounce it, and he began to practise using "this" and "then" in place of "dis" and "den."

"There!" exclaimed Jimmy triumphantly one night as he looked at a piece of paper. "There's me name!" and he looked at it proudly, for it was written after a severe effort on his part. "Did I speak right den—I mean then?" he asked.

"Very nearly, except that you said 'me name' instead of 'my name', Jimmy."

"Dat's so—I mean that's so. Well, what do youse think of me—I mean my writin'?"

"It's very good; but if you want to speak correctly, don't say 'youse' for you, and put a final 'g' on your words that need it."

"Crimps! but dat's—I mean that's a lot to remember," he answered with a sigh.

"You're not sorry you're learning, though, are you?"

"Betcher life I ain't."

He gave a sudden start.

"I s'pose I shouldn't say that," he added.

"Well, I don't know that it's any particular harm," answered Dick. "It's slang, and when you grow up to be a man I don't suppose you'll like to use slang. The trouble is, as I've read, it's hard to break off the habit. So I suppose it's best to start young."

"Dat's—I mean that's what it is. I'm goin'—there, I dropped another 'g'—I'm going to try," and Jimmy spoke very slowly.

"You're doing very well," complimented his young teacher. "I wish I was making some progress myself."

"What do you mean?"

"I mean I'd like to find out who I am. Sometimes in the night I get to thinking about it, and I feel quite badly. I think I must have some—some folks somewhere, and maybe they're anxious about me."

50

"Don't any of it come back to youse—I mean you?" asked Jimmy sympathetically.

"Not the least. I've tried and tried again, but all I can remember is a big house somewhere with lots of ground around it and a man and a lady who were good to me. I seem to remember driving a horse once."

"Maybe you worked as a driver," suggested Jimmy, "and a horse kicked you. That's how your head was hurt, maybe."

"I don't believe so. I don't remember working anywhere. I wish there was some way of finding out about myself."

Jimmy felt a sudden twinge of his conscience. Perhaps it was his fault that Dick had not been able to discover the secret of the mystery that surrounded him. Jimmy had said nothing to the police about the boy, and Sam Schmidt had not read of any reward being offered for information of a missing lad. Jimmy determined to make amends.

"Dick, I've got somethin' to tell you," he said, speaking slowly and more correctly than he ever talked before. "Maybe it's my fault that you don't know who you are."

"Your fault? How do you mean?"

And then Jimmy, feeling very much ashamed of himself, told of how he had kept silent, hoping that a reward would be offered.

"I'm—I'm awful sorry," he concluded. "I feel real mean about it, Dick, for you've been so good to me an' have done so much for me."

For a few seconds Dick said nothing. The disclosure was quite a shock to him. But he did not blame Jimmy, for he realized that the boy did not know any better.

"Do you think the police would know anything about me, Jimmy?" asked Dick at length.

"Maybe they would. Come on, we'll go to headquarters," replied Jimmy, anxious to make up for lost time.

It did not take the two boys long to reach police headquarters in Mulberry Street. Jimmy felt a little diffident about going into that dreaded place, of which he had heard so much, and the brass-buttoned sergeant sitting behind the brass railing looked very stern, but the newsboy mustered up courage to enter. As for Dick, he was filled with a nervous excitement.

The story was soon told, and the sergeant at once took an interest in Dick's queer plight. He questioned the youth carefully, but, as we know, Dick could tell little about himself. The sergeant went over the books from the time Jimmy had found his partner in the box, but there was no report of any missing boys answering the description of Dick, though there were many youngsters missing.

"Didn't you say you had a hat with you in the box?" asked the sergeant.

"Yes, sir," replied Dick. "That is it," and he handed it over.

The officer looked at the band inside. This was a bit of detective work that had not occurred to either Dick or Jimmy.

51

"Hum!" remarked the sergeant with a shake of his head. "All it says is 'Boston Store.' I thought it might give the name of the place where it was bought."

"Perhaps it was purchased in Boston," suggested Dick, "though I don't remember ever living near there."

"No," replied the officer, "nearly every city has either a 'New York' or a 'Boston' or a 'Philadelphia' store, and they are scattered from here to San Francisco. It's a queer custom. If that hat had the maker's name in it it might be a clue. However, I'll telegraph to Boston and make some inquiries."

"When will you have an answer?" asked Dick eagerly.

"Some time to-morrow, or maybe late to-night. Better call in to-morrow."

"I will," promised Dick, and feeling for the first time since he found himself in this queer plight that there was a ray of hope, he and Jimmy went back to the lodging-house.

Dick did not sleep well that night, for he was thinking that perhaps the next day would find his identity established and the mystery solved.

CHAPTER XV

PITCHING PENNIES

But Dick was doomed to disappointment. Early the next morning he and Jimmy called at police headquarters.

"There's no news for you," said the sergeant. "I wired to Boston, but the police there haven't any calls for any missing boys answering your description. If you were a man now you might answer."

"Why, are there any men missing?" asked Dick, interested to know there were other persons in a similar plight to his own.

"Yes, several. However, don't be discouraged. I'll keep on the lookout, and if I hear anything I'll let you know. Better leave me your address."

Dick gave it to the sergeant and then, rather discouraged, he left with Jimmy to begin the day's work of selling papers.

"I guess nobody wants me back," said Dick a little sadly as, with his bundle under his arm, he started for Wall Street.

"Sure they does," declared Jimmy. "It'll come out all right, you see. Anyhow, I want you. I don't know what I'd a' done if it hadn't been fer youse—I mean for you."

"Oh, I guess you'd have gotten along," replied Dick, smiling to see his partner's efforts to talk more correctly. "However, I'm glad I'm of some use to some one. I hope we have a good day to-day so we can put some more money in the bank."

"Ain't we got quite a lot?"

"Yes, but I want to get enough ahead for a special purpose."

"What is it?"

"I'll tell you later. It's going to be a surprise."

Then, fearing Jimmy would ask more questions, Dick hurried off.

Business was fair the rest of the week, and Saturday night Jimmy and Dick were able to put away three dollars between them.

"Come on," said Dick that night after supper.

"Where you going?"

"To the bank."

"You don't need me to put that money in."

"No, but I'm going to draw some out."

"Draw some out? What fer—I mean what for?"

"You're going to have a new suit of clothes," declared Dick. "You need one, and we can afford it. That is not exactly a new one, but I saw some good second-handed clothes in a store to-day, cheap, and you need a suit."

"I guess I do," admitted Jimmy, looking at his rather ragged one. "But it ain't fair to take the money for that. We may need it."

"If we do we'll earn more. You have a right to look as good as possible, now that we're in business. It will make a better impression on the customers."

"Dat's so—I mean that's so," agreed Jimmy. "Well, I'll leave it to you."

They went to the bank, which kept open Saturday night for the benefit of depositors who got their wages on that day, and Dick drew out enough, with what they had accumulated that week, to buy Jimmy a good second-hand suit. The boy's appearance was much improved by it, and he surveyed himself proudly.

The purchase of the suit made quite a little hole in their savings, but Dick did not regret it. For the first time since he and Jimmy had been partners they went walking the following Sunday in the better part of the city. Heretofore Jimmy, with his ragged garments, had refused to stir away from the vicinity of the lodging-house, but now he felt that even Fifth Avenue was not too stylish for him. Certainly clothes make a great difference to almost any one.

Dick, who had a dim recollection of having been in the habit of going to church on Sunday, wanted to propose it to Jimmy, but he reasoned that the newsboy might object to having too many reforms instituted at once. So Dick decided to wait a while.

Several weeks passed, and Jimmy continued to improve in his lessons. He could write short sentences now, and was beginning to be able to read simple stories in an old school book Dick had purchased. The young teacher also began to impart to his pupil a knowledge of arithmetic, and this he found was comparatively easy, as Jimmy had a good head for figures and was quick in making change.

Prosperity seemed to smile on the two newsboy partners. They continued to save a little every week, and in this they were encouraged by Mr. Snowden, manager of the lodging-house. Frank Merton, whose room was not far from where the two boys had theirs, used frequently to come in evenings and help Jimmy with his lessons. As Dick had a good education, he was also of service to Frank, who had had to leave school when very young.

"Why don't you get ready to go to night school when the term opens, Jimmy?" proposed Frank one night.

"Maybe I will."

"That would be a good thing," agreed Dick. "I think I'll go myself."

"You? You don't want to learn any more, do you?" asked Jimmy, whose language had improved very much.

"Indeed I do. Why, I don't know much more than you do. I must have been going to school—in my—before the accident happened, you know," for that was the way Dick referred to the past.

"If we all three could go it would be fine," said Frank. "They have good teachers at the school where I go. The term will open again in September. That's about two months off."

The boys discussed this plan, and Dick, though he did not mention it, had it in mind to propose to Jimmy soon that they take Frank into partnership with them. Dick's trade in papers in the financial district was growing to such an extent that he could scarcely take care of all his customers, with the limited number of papers he could carry. He was thinking of opening a stand in Wall Street if he saw a chance for a good location. But he decided to wait a while.

In the meanwhile the police sergeant had received no word concerning Dick, and the boy was much disappointed. However, he kept up his courage as best he could, hoping something would occur to disclose his identity and put him in communication with his relatives, if he had any. He and Frank kept close watch of the reward and personal columns of the papers, and Jimmy, whose reading had rapidly improved, also did as much as he was able to in this respect.

Dick was beginning to feel proud of his success with Jimmy, and the teacher, young as he was, began to perceive that the newsboy had a sterling character. It is true that once or twice Jimmy had forgotten his promise about smoking, and when out with other boys of his acquaintance had indulged in a cigarette or two. But he was always sorry for these lapses, and after telling Dick of them would make a new resolve. He had not smoked now in over three weeks. He was using less and less slang, too, and his manners were much improved.

These changes and the wearing of neater clothes could not but have their effect. Though his former companions laughed at the changes in Jimmy, he knew they were doing him good. He began to assume a more business-like air.

"Well, well!" exclaimed Mr. Crosscrab one day as he stopped to buy a paper of Jimmy. "Matters seem to be going pretty well with you. You look prosperous."

"We're doing fine!" declared Jimmy. "It's all due to me—I mean my—partner, though. He's all to de merry—I mean he's a fine lad."

"I must call and see him," said the young man. "I should like to meet such a sensible business boy, as you tell me he is. Perhaps I could help him, as I am thinking of going into business myself here in New York."

"Say, don't bust up—I mean break up our partnership," pleaded Jimmy. "I wouldn't know what to do now without Dick."

"Yes, I guess it would be a pity to separate you. Well, I'll not do it."

But if Dick expected Jimmy was going to improve all at once, and drop all his manners and customs learned of a long association with street urchins, he was disappointed. One day, when Dick came up from Wall Street a little earlier than usual, he went to Barclay Street and Broadway to look for Jimmy. He did not find him there as he expected.

"Seen Jimmy?" he asked of Sam Schmidt, who was standing there selling papers.

"Yah. He und Ted Snook, dey iss gone off."

"Gone off? Where?"

"Hush! Don't say nottings, but Jimmy he ask me t' take his place und sell vot babers he had left."

"What did he do that for?"

"Hush! He und Ted, dey is goin' t' pitch pennies."

"Pitch pennies?"

"Yah! Down by der Battery, vere dere ain't no cobs. Der cobs 'ud arrest 'em if dey ketched 'em, so dey vent down dere. Ted he sait as how he could beat Jimmy, und Jimmy says as how he can vin all Ted's pennies. So dey are at it, und I is sellin' Jimmy's babers."

"Pitching pennies!" exclaimed Dick to himself, with a little sinking of his heart. "I hope Jimmy doesn't do much of that gambling. If he gets in with that crowd he'll begin smoking again. I must go after him." And he started toward the Battery to look for his erring partner.

CHAPTER XVI

THE DOCTOR'S VERDICT

Dick did not have to ask any directions to find Jimmy when he reached the Battery, which, as most of my readers may know, is a small park at the lower end of the metropolis. He saw a crowd of lads gathered in a secluded corner, and he at once knew them to be newsboys and bootblacks, for he recognized a number of them.

"That's where they are probably pitching pennies," he thought. "I must get Jimmy away from there."

His approach was unnoticed, so intent were the lads on the game, and not until Dick called Jimmy's name was the latter aware that his partner was present. Even then, beyond a first start of surprise, he showed no astonishment.

"Hello, Dick," he called. "How'd you find me?"

"Sam Schmidt told me."

"Sam Schmidt! I'll punch his head fer squealin' on us!" exclaimed a red-haired lad. "What right's he got t' butt in?"

"That's all right," responded Jimmy with an air of superior knowledge. "He's a partner of mine. Dick's all right. Did you want me, Dick?"

"Yes, you'd better come with me."

"Aw, an' break up de game!" expostulated several. "Why, Jimmy is winners, an' he can't go until we gits our stakes out."

"Sure I'm winnin'!" said Jimmy proudly. "I'm forty-two cents to the good now."

"I'd like to talk to you," went on Dick to his chum.

"All right, I'll come."

"Naw; stay!" called Pete Lanson. "Here, have a cigarette, Bricks."

Jimmy stretched out his hand to take one of the paper and tobacco rolls. For an instant he forgot his promise to Dick. Then he remembered it and shook his head.

"Gee! Youse must 'a' turned inter a Sunday-school kid," sneered Pete.

"I cut out smokin'," declared Jimmy, with a slight blush. "Me an' me partner can't afford it," he went on. "We're savin'—I mean saving—up for to buy a regular stand."

"Git on t' his sassiry language!" remarked another, with a mean laugh. "Fust we know Bricks'll be shakin' us all togedder."

"Dat's right," chimed in one or two.

"Go on, Bricks; it's your shot," advised Pete. "I t'ink I kin win from youse now."

"Are you coming with me?" asked Dick in a low tone.

"Say, kid, be youse his guardian?" inquired a big lad. "Why didn't youse tie a string t' Bricks if yer so careful of him as all dat."

"Guess I'll have to go, fellers," spoke up Jimmy, rather regretfully, it must be admitted.

"What? An' not give us a chance t' git some of our money back?" came from three or four.

"Some other day I will."

"Naw, I want t' pitch some more now," declared Pete.

There were angry murmurs at Dick's interference, and several scowled at Jimmy. It looked as if there might be trouble, but just then a policeman opportunely came in sight. Some one spied him, and there was a cry:

"Cheese it, de cop!"

Instantly the penny-pitching crowd dispersed as if by magic. Most of the boys jumped through the railings, cut across the grass plots and were lost to sight among the trees. The bigger lads walked more slowly, with an assumed air of innocence. As for Jimmy, he joined Dick, and the two strolled over to the edge of the Battery wall, looking down into the swirling waters of the bay.

"Did you want anything special?" asked Jimmy.

"Yes, I did."

"What is it? Is there a big extra out?"

"No. I heard you were gambling, and I came down to stop you."

"Gambling? You don't call pitchin' pennies gambling, do you, Dick?"

"What else is it?"

"Well, I s'pose it is, in a way. But that's no harm. All the fellows does it."

"I'm afraid that doesn't make it good, Jimmy. I don't want to be finding fault all the while, and I'm sure I don't set up to be any better than you are, but I know gambling is bad. You'll never win in the long run, and it will do you harm. Besides, you can't afford to lose, even if it is not wrong."

"But I won to-day."

"Do you often win?"

"Naw, this is the first time I ever made much. Most times I lose."

"I thought so. I hope you don't do it much."

"Not very often. De cops—I mean the policemen—are too strict. I do it once in a while."

"I wish you'd give it up," went on Dick. "I know I'm asking a lot of you. First you gave up smoking for me, then the use of slang and rough expressions, and now I ask you this. But I do it for your own good and because I like you, Jimmy."

"I know youse does—I mean you do, Dick, an'—say—I'll—I'll stop pitching pennies if you don't like it."

"Will you, really?"

"Honest! Here's my hand!"

Jimmy was thoroughly in earnest, and Dick knew his partner would keep his word. It might be well to say right here that from then on Jimmy never gambled, though often he was sorely tempted by his associates.

"What'd I better do with this money?" asked Jimmy after a pause. "I s'pose if it ain't right t' pitch pennies, it ain't right t' keep the money."

"No, it is not. Do you know who you won it from?"

"Sure."

"Then I'd give it back."

"Well, I guess I will, but it comes hard. I was goin' to a good show to-night with it."

"I'll stand treat for the show," said Dick, for he felt that something was coming to Jimmy for giving in about the gambling.

57

"Bully fer youse—I mean that's fine! But I've got t' pay Sam Schmidt for selling papers for me."

"Yes, you will be a little out of pocket on account of taking the time off, but better that than to get in the habit of gambling."

"Well, I didn't do so much, and I never thought it was wrong. All the fellers does it."

"I suppose so, but if we're going to make a success of this business we can't afford to gamble."

"No, I s'pose not," replied Jimmy a little dubiously.

Dick took his partner to a better class of theatrical performance that night, for the lad who had forgotten his identity did not care much for the moving picture shows.

"How do you like this?" he asked Jimmy.

"Well," was the slow answer, "I s'pose it's swell, an' all that, an' I'll get used to it in time, but I like a prize-fight best."

Dick laughed heartily, but he did not tell his partner the cause of his mirth.

During the days that followed the two newsboys did a good business. They sold many papers, and Dick was now on an equal footing with Jimmy, though the latter had had much more experience. There was more talk of taking Frank Merton into partnership with them, but as the latter had built up a good trade for himself in another part of the city, he did not know whether it would be a wise thing or not to make a new venture.

Meanwhile Dick was no nearer a solution of the mystery than enshrouded him. Night after night he would try and try again to remember who he was and where he came from, but without result. The past was like a sealed book to him, and he had absolutely no recollection of who he was or where he had lived.

"Do you know what I would do?" said Frank one night when, in the room of the partners, the three were talking over the strange case.

"Well, what would you do, Frank?" asked Jimmy.

"I'd take Dick to a doctor."

"A doctor? Why, I'm not sick!" exclaimed Dick.

"No, I suppose not. But I read of a case the other day of a man who was hit on the head and he forgot everything he ever knew. They took him to a hospital, operated on him, and his memory came back to him."

"I wonder if mine would?" asked Dick, with a new look of hope on his face.

"There's nothing like trying," said Frank. "Suppose we ask the superintendent, Mr. Snowden?"

"That's a good idea," came from Jimmy, who was sitting in a corner of the room.

This they did, and Mr. Snowden agreed to have a physician who was a friend of his look at Dick. The superintendent of the lodging-house agreed, in a measure, with Frank that perhaps there might be some injury to Dick's head because of the blow, which, when the resulting depression on the skull was removed, would bring back his memory.

A few days later the doctor examined Dick. The boy waited anxiously for the verdict.

"I am sorry," said the doctor, "but I can do nothing for you. There is no special injury to the head. The skull was not broken by whatever, or whoever, it was that hit you. You suffered some shock, and that took away your memory. Your mind now is as good as it was before the accident, except that everything in the past is blotted out."

"And will I never remember it again?" asked Dick.

"I would not say that. The chances are that some day it will all come back to you with a rush. Some forgotten incident will recall it all to you. It may be a slight thing—the hearing of some forgotten name—the seeing of some forgotten face—and then you may remember who you are and where you lived."

"Oh, I hope it comes soon," said poor Dick. "I am tired of all this uncertainty."

"Never mind," consoled Jimmy. "I'll stick by you to the last."

CHAPTER XVII

AN OFFER OF A STAND

The disappointment following the doctor's verdict was keen for Dick. He had hoped that something might be done to aid him, but he found the only thing he could do was to wait, and this was very tedious.

"And maybe it will never happen," he said to Jimmy, that night in their room.

"Yes, it will," declared his partner, with more conviction that he felt. "You'll remember who you are some day, I'm certain."

"Perhaps—when it's too late."

"Well, don't think any more about it," advised Jimmy. "I heard some news to-day I forgot to tell you."

"What was it?"

"Well, a fellow that has a fine news-stand on Sixth Avenue near the elevated road wants to sell out. He's sick, an' he's got to go out West. I thought maybe you and me could buy him out."

"That's so, we might. How much does he want?"

"I don't know. Sam Schmidt was telling me about it. I didn't see the man who owns it."

"Suppose we go and see him," suggested Dick.

It had, for some time, been the ambition of the newsboy partners to own a regular stand, where not only papers but magazines and weeklies could be sold. Jimmy, in his wildest ambition, had sometimes dreamed of such a rise in life,

59

but, until he had met Dick and learned new habits, including the one of saving his money, such a thing had not been possible for him, even to consider. Now he hoped he was in a position to realize his fondest expectation.

They went to see the owner of the stand the next day. The location, they knew from their past experience, was a good one, as it was near several ferries and street-car lines, as well as right under an elevated station. Thus the owner of the stand could always be assured of a large number of customers.

"I wonder how much he'll want for it?" spoke Dick, as they approached.

"Oh, maybe about forty or fifty dollars. How much have we got saved up now?"

"Nearly twenty-five."

"Maybe he'll trust us for what we haven't got, Dick."

"Perhaps, if we give him a mortgage."

"What's a mortgage?"

"Why, it's a paper showing that you owe a man so much money, and you give him a claim on your property as security. You'll soon learn about them in your arithmetic, especially when we get going to night-school."

"I don't care whether I learn or not, if I can be a part-owner in that stand," declared Jimmy, his eyes shining as he noted the pile of papers and magazines and saw the little enclosure where the proprietor of the place sat.

"Oh, but you must," insisted Dick. "Now shall I do the talking, or will you?"

"You'd better. But if he tries to come any 'con' game on us I'll have something to say. I know lots about selling papers, but not much about buying stands."

"I hear this stand is for sale," began Dick, speaking to a young man in charge.

"Who told you?" was the somewhat suspicious answer.

"My partner here, James Small, heard it from another newsboy, Sam Schmidt. Isn't it correct?"

"I suppose it is. I want to sell out. I've got to go West for my lungs."

"That's too bad. How much do you want for the stand?"

"Well, you know this is a good place to do business."

"I'll have to take your word for it," replied Dick. "Still it seems quite a lively place and ought to be good."

"Good? I guess it is!"

"How much do youse—I mean you—take in every week?" asked Jimmy suddenly, for he felt he could safely ask this question.

"What's that got to do with it?" inquired the stand-owner sharply.

"Lots. If me and me partner buys this stand, we want to know how much we're going to make."

"Well, I do a good business. Of course some days it's better than others."

"What does it average?" asked Dick.

"Well," replied the proprietor, after some figuring, "it averages fifty-five dollars a week."

Jimmy uttered a low whistle of surprise. That was higher than he had thought.

"And what are the expenses?" asked Dick quietly.

"I have to pay the elevated railroad company ten dollars a week for having my stand here, and I have to hire a boy to bring me papers and other supplies, for I sell cigars and tobacco. But there aren't many weeks when I don't clear twenty dollars."

Dick thought this was a fine business, but, of course, if he and Jimmy took it there would not be so much profit for each of them as the man got, unless they could increase the business. That was another matter to consider.

"How much do you want for the stand?" asked Dick, while he and Jimmy waited anxiously for the answer.

"Well, I'll take two hundred and fifty dollars cash, and not a cent less."

The figure was so high, and the announcement of it caused the partners such a surprise, that, for a moment, they did not know what to say.

CHAPTER XVIII

BULLDOG THREATENS DICK

Dick was the first to recover his composure. He had to admit that he had no idea of what a news-stand in New York might be worth. His previous notions, as well as those of Jimmy, had evidently been wrong.

"I'm afraid that figure is too high for us," spoke Dick slowly.

"High? That's dirt cheap," declared the young man. "Why you can make the stand pay for itself in six months. I'd never give it up if it wasn't that my health has failed."

"But we haven't got that much money," said Dick frankly.

"Can't you get it somewhere?"

"I'm afraid not. You see we are in partnership. We haven't been at it very long, but we've managed to save up twenty-five dollars."

"Oh, I couldn't think of taking that and waiting for the rest," declared the stand-owner.

"No, I wouldn't expect you to."

"Maybe you could borrow the rest somewhere. I'd be willing to take two hundred in cash and a mortgage for the balance."

"That would mean we'd have to borrow one hundred and seventy-five dollars somewhere," said Dick. "No, we can't think of it. We'll have to look for a cheaper stand or wait until we have more money saved up."

"You'll never get a cheaper stand. I know something about them, for I tried to buy one when I first went in the business."

"I haven't any doubt but what this stand is worth all you ask for it," went on Dick, "but it's beyond our means. I'm sorry."

"So am I," frankly admitted the young man. "I'd like to sell out to a couple of young fellows, but, of course, if you haven't the money you can't do business. And I need cash to go away with."

"Well, we'll have to look somewhere else," remarked Jimmy, much disappointed. They bade the young man good-bye and started back to resume the selling of papers, which they had interrupted in order to make their inquiries.

"Did you think he'd want so much as that?" asked Jimmy, as they walked up Barclay Street.

"No, I hadn't any idea stands were worth so much."

"Me either. I guess we'll never get one now."

"Yes, we will," declared Dick firmly. "I'm going to have one. If we can't find a cheaper one, we'll save up more money. A stand is the only way to make a good living in this business."

"Oh, we've done pretty well," observed Jimmy. "I've made more money since I've been with you than I ever made before."

"Yes, but it's not enough for a firm like ours," and Dick laughed. "We want to do three times as much."

During the days that followed the two partners devoted themselves harder than ever to the business of selling papers. They did well, too, for Jimmy had much improved in his methods and had attracted a number of new customers, who regularly bought their papers from him. Dick, also, had increased his trade and was becoming well known in the financial district as "the polite newsboy."

While at first there had been, on the part of other lads selling papers, a disposition to annoy Dick, they now let him alone. One reason for this was a quiet word spoken to the policeman in that district by one or two brokers, who had taken a liking to Dick, and who understood the opposition to him. After that the officer kept his eyes open and, having threatened to arrest several lads who annoyed the newcomer, there was no more trouble.

Meanwhile Dick was no nearer than ever a solution of the mystery that surrounded him. He hoped nothing now from the police, and, as for seeing some notice in the papers describing a missing boy like himself, he had long ago given that up. The two partners continued to live in their room at the lodging-house, and they were slowly accumulating a nice little balance in the bank.

But it grew slowly, too slowly to give them hope that they would reach the figure demanded by the news-stand owner in time to buy him out.

They heard, incidentally, that several of the bigger newsboys were thinking of consolidating and purchasing the place, and Jimmy suggested that he and Dick take Frank into partnership, but when the matter was explained to him, Frank, while grateful for the offer, said he could not afford to go into the scheme. He had some money saved up, but he said he had to help support a widowed aunt, a sister of his dead mother, and, as she would soon have to undergo an operation in the institution where she was, he was saving his money to help pay for it, as the old lady was destitute.

So that practically shattered the hopes of the two partners of owning the stand. Nor could they find one any cheaper that would suit their purpose.

"Never mind," said Dick. "We'll be ready to buy one next year."

But if Dick had ceased, save at odd times, to make some effort at discovering his identity, this was not true of two other persons. These were Bulldog Smouder and Mike Conroy. The two plotters had not forgotten their plan.

"Say, Bulldog," said Mike, one night not long after Dick's and Jimmy's attempt to buy the stand, "ain't dere nuttin' doin' in gittin' de reward fer dat kid?"

"Sure dere is."

"What?"

"Well, I've got me plans all made."

"'Bout time youse said somethin'. Did de detective know anyt'ing?"

"Not a t'ing. Dere ain't been no reward offered."

"Den what's de good of bodderin' wid it?"

"Dis good. I'm satisfied dat kid run away from home somewhere a good ways off. Dat's why nuttin' ain't been heard of it here in N'York. But I'll bet his folks, whoever dey are, wants him back. He's one of dem nice kids. He ain't fit fer dis business."

"He seems t' sell a lot of papers," remarked Mike.

"Yep. Too many. I'd like t' git him outer de way an' I could make more money down Wall Street way. So if we kin find out where he belongs we'll git de reward an' business'll be better fer us."

"Dat's so. How youse goin' t' do it?"

"Listen, an' I'll tell ye."

Then the two cronies whispered together for come time.

"Dat's a good plan," said Mike at length. "I'll do me share. When youse goin' t' try it?"

"T'-night. Once youse gits Jimmy outer de way de rest'll be plain sailin' fer me."

"Oh, I'll do it."

Soon after this the two plotters separated. Meanwhile Dick and Jimmy, all unconscious of what was being planned against them, were doing business as usual.

When Dick got back to the room, late that afternoon, having been out selling extras after their regular work in the financial district, he was surprised not to find Jimmy. He had seen the latter, not an hour before, and his partner had said he was, even then, on his way to the lodging-house to get ready for supper. Jimmy had promised to wait for Dick.

"I hope he hasn't gone off with some of those boys, pitching pennies," thought Dick. For he never could be quite sure of Jimmy, who was easily tempted, though, of late, he had been very good indeed.

But Dick's wonderment over his chum's absence was cut short by the entrance of Bulldog into the room, when, in answer to a knock on the door, Dick had called an invitation to enter.

"Evenin'," said Bulldog shortly. "Jimmy sent me fer youse, Dick. He want's youse t' come."

"Jimmy wants me? Where is he? What has happened?"

Dick felt a sudden fear.

"He's hurted a little bit—not much," went on Bulldog, "and he was took inter a house. He wants youse t' come. Will yer?"

"Of course. Do you know where he is?"

"Sure. I seen him a while ago. He ain't hurt bad. If youse'll come wit' me I'll show youse."

"Wait until I get my coat on and I'll come with you."

Dick followed his former enemy out of the lodging-house. He had no reason to suspect anything, for, of late, Bulldog had been rather friendly than otherwise.

Dick followed his guide into one of the worst parts of New York, but had little fear, as he had, more or less, become used to traveling about the slums with Jimmy. Bulldog led the way down through a dirty alley and into a ramschackle tenement.

"He's right upstairs," he said. "Come on."

Dick followed in the semi-darkness, illuminated by only a flaring kerosene lamp. Bulldog went into a room, and Dick, expecting to see his partner lying hurt on a bed or lounge, was surprised to see no one in the place.

"Why—why—where's Jimmy?" he asked.

"Jimmy is over in Brooklyn," said Bulldog, with a laugh.

"In Brooklyn? I thought you said he was hurt."

"Well, I guess he is, fer he's bound t' fight wid Mike when he finds out he's been fooled, an' Mike's liable t' hurt him."

"But what for? Why should he be in Brooklyn? And why have you brought me here?"

"Jimmy's in Brooklyn t' git him outer de way," explained Bulldog, with an ugly leer, "an' youse is here t' answer me some questions. Now, den, kid, I wants t' know where youse run away from home, who youse be, an' where youse lives. I'm goin' t' take youse back an' git de reward. Now youse can't fool me, an' if youse tries, it'll be bad fer yer. Come now, own up. Didn't youse run away from home? Answer me or I'll punch ye till yer does!" and Bulldog threateningly shook his fist in Dick's face.

"Didn't youse run away from home?" Page 137

CHAPTER XIX

JIMMY TO THE RESCUE

When Jimmy started for the room, late that afternoon, after having met Dick and arranging to go to supper with him, he was accosted, just before he reached the lodging-house, by Mike Conroy. Now, though Jimmy suspected Mike of having robbed him, and though he considered him his enemy, Jimmy was a whole-souled, good-hearted lad, not long holding enmity against any one. So, when Mike greeted him pleasantly enough, Jimmy responded in kind.

"Heard youse was lookin' fer a news-stand t' buy," said Mike.

"We was," replied Jimmy, "but it was too steep for us."

"I know a feller what's got one t' sell cheap."

"Where?"

"Over in Brooklyn."

"I don't believe we'd like to go to Brooklyn. New York is the best place for a newspaper stand. You can make more money here."

"No, I mean de feller what owns it lives in Brooklyn. De stand is in New York, close t' de elevated."

"How much does he want for it?"

"About seventy-five dollars."

This was so near the figure that he and Dick could command that Jimmy was at once interested.

"What's the man's address?" he asked.

"I'll take youse t' him," volunteered Mike. "He said he'd pay me a commission if I brought him a customer, an' I'll bring youse."

"All right. I'll go. But I must leave word for Dick where I'm gone."

"Oh, youse needn't bodder about dat. We'll soon be back," said Mike quickly. "Come on."

So, thinking he would return almost as soon as his partner reached the room, Jimmy went away with Mike. They crossed the bridge in the cars, Mike generously paying the fares, and, once on the Brooklyn side, Mike led the way to a trolley. They rode for some time, and finally Jimmy exclaimed:

"I thought you said it was only a little ways. We're out in the country now."

"We're most there," declared Mike quickly. "It's only a few minutes now," and he began to talk rapidly, telling Jimmy a number of stories of New York life, and so keeping his companion interested to that extent that Jimmy did not notice how far they had come.

"We'll git out here," said Mike, at length.

"Say, this is the country for fair," exclaimed Jimmy, as he found himself in the midst of open fields with only a few houses here and there. "This feller must want to get a good ways off from his work."

"He does. It's jest a short walk now."

It was getting dusk and Jimmy was beginning to think Dick would get tired of waiting for him. He began to wish he had left some word, or else that he had not gone with Mike. The latter led the way across the fields, toward a house.

"Look out!" suddenly exclaimed Jimmy's companion. The boy turned his head, and the next instant he felt one of Mike's arms encircle his neck, while with the other hand Mike held Jimmy's wrists in a firm grip. Then, before Jimmy knew what was happening, Mike took his arm from his neck and plunged that hand into Jimmy's pocket where the newsboy kept his money. He was robbing Jimmy.

"Here! Let up! Quit that! Police!" cried the smaller boy, struggling to free himself. But Mike was too strong for him, and, in that lonely place, there were no officers. It was growing quite dark and no help was in sight.

Suddenly Mike withdrew his hand from Jimmy's pocket, bringing out with it all the money. Then, giving the smaller lad a push that sent him stumbling to the ground, Mike turned and ran away, making for the distant trolley line.

"Now youse kin walk home, Bricks!" he called. "Youse'll git dere by t'-morror mornin'."

"Give me back my money!" shouted Jimmy, scrambling to his feet.

Mike, with a mocking laugh, raced on. He was too swift a runner for Jimmy, but the smaller boy pluckily kept after him. Mike had a good lead, and a little later he reached the trolley line and jumped aboard a passing car, which soon took him out of sight.

"Well, if that ain't a mean trick!" exclaimed Jimmy, pausing when he saw it was useless to run farther. "He brought me out here to rob me. I wonder what he did that for? There's lots of places in New York. I wonder——" then a sudden thought came to him.

"Dick!" he exclaimed. "Maybe they're going to do something to him and they wanted to get me out of the way. That's it! They're up to some trick, Mike and Bulldog, I'll bet anything! And me many miles from New York and not a cent of car fare!" he added ruefully, as he felt in all his pockets. Mike had done his part well and had taken every cent Jimmy had.

For a time the boy did not know what to do. He realized that he must hurry back to the lodging-house, but how to reach there was another question. He thought of getting on a trolley car, telling the conductor his plight, and asking for free transportation. Then there was his fare to pay across the bridge, though, of course, he could walk. For that matter he could tramp the entire distance, but it would take him quite a while; and, meanwhile, what might happen to Dick? He felt rather dubious about asking the trolley car conductor to trust him. Probably the man would not believe his story.

"I certainly am up against it good and hard!" said Jimmy to himself.

Rapidly he considered matters. Then, as he saw a light shining from a distant house, he made up his mind to ask for help. He thought over what he had better say, and then, determining to be bold, as the case demanded, he rang the bell and asked for the loan of ten cents, as that was all he needed to get home.

"I'll leave you my watch for security," went on Jimmy, after he had explained to the lady some of the circumstances of the case. "It's only a dollar one, but it's new and it keeps good time."

67

Fortunately Jimmy had approached a kind woman, who had a boy of her own, and she not only loaned him the ten cents, but fifteen more, giving him a quarter. Nor would she take the watch as security. Jimmy promised to return the money the next day, and then, profuse in his thanks, he hurried for the trolley and caught a car for Brooklyn Bridge.

Arriving at the lodging-house he hurried to the apartment. His worst fears were realized. Dick was gone, and, from the appearance of the room, he had left in a hurry, for his things were scattered around.

"They've got him!" exclaimed Jimmy in despair. "Guess I'd better tell the police."

He questioned Mr. Snowden, but the manager had not seen Dick depart with Bulldog. Nor was he inclined to think that anything had occurred. He suggested that Dick had gone out to take a walk, but Jimmy felt that something had happened.

He went out into the street, hardly knowing what to do, but trying to make up his mind to some plan of action. He saw Sam Schmidt, and, more because he could think of no one else to appeal to than because he hoped for news, he asked:

"Seen Dick this evenin', Dutchy?"

"Sure, dot's vot I has," was the unexpected answer.

"You have? Where?"

"Him und Bulldog Smouder vent off over towards de Bowery a while ago. Und dey vos in a hurry-up I d'inks, for dey vos valkin' fast."

"Where does Bulldog live?"

Sam gave the required information.

"Will you come with me, Dutchy?" asked Jimmy eagerly.

"Vere to?"

Jimmy rapidly explained and expressed his belief that Bulldog had enticed Dick away somewhere, though what his object could be he could hardly guess.

"Sure, I goes mit youse," declared the German newsboy. "Ve lick dot Bulldogs feller, dot's vot ve does."

"I guess we can manage him between us," said Jimmy, as he and Sam started off to rescue Dick.

CHAPTER XX

DICK IS ILL

When Dick saw that he had been fooled by Bulldog and was in the power of the bully, his first thought was one of fear. For Dick was not a very strong lad and was unused to physical violence. So, when the big lad shook his fist in his face and appeared ready to strike him Dick shrank back.

"Aw, I t'ought I'd skeer youse," remarked Bulldog in surly tones. "Now youse had better tell me a straight story."

"What do you mean?" asked Dick.

"Aw, youse know what I means. Youse has run away from home an' ye're only chuckin' a bluff about bein' a newsboy. Now I want t' know where youse lives, so's I kin take youse home an' git der reward."

"If I knew where I lived and who my folks were, I would only be too glad to tell you," answered Dick earnestly. "I would go home myself, without waiting for any one to take me."

"None of dat. Dat's too thin!" exclaimed Bulldog. "Youse has got t' tell me or I'll punch yer head."

"I can't tell you."

"Well, den here goes fer a punch," and again the big boy raised his big fist.

"I'll call a policeman," said Dick, who knew he was no match for the bully.

"Go ahead. We lick cops down dis way. No perliceman ever comes in here when he hears a row. He knows it ain't healthy fer him, 'less he's got a patrol wagon full of cops wid him. Now, once ag'in, are youse goin' t' tell me what I want t' know?"

"I can't!" exclaimed Dick, wishing he had Jimmy there to help him. "I would, really I would, if I could, but I can't remember anything, except that I got hit on the head and then I woke up in the box with Jimmy."

"Yes, dat's de story youse tells, but I t'ink it's a fake. What I want is de real t'ing."

"I am telling you the truth."

"Well, I don't believe youse are."

"You can ask the police at headquarters. I have been there and told them my story."

"Yes; when youse catches me around police headquarters it'll be colder dan it is now."

Bulldog grasped Dick by an arm and pulled him closer to him, while his heavy fist was ready to deal a cruel blow. Dick tried to shrink away, but he was held fast. He looked about the room for some way of escape or some weapon he might use on his captor.

The apartment, as far as he could see in the dim light of a smoking oil lamp, was deserted. There was only one door, that by which they had entered, and Bulldog had locked that. Nor was there anything in the room, save a table and a few chairs.

"Oh, youse can't git away from me," said Bulldog, guessing of what Dick was thinking. "Now, den, take dat!" and he dealt Dick a hard blow in the face. Instinctively the boy raised his arm to protect his head.

"Oh, youse wants t' fight, eh?" inquired the bully, with a sneer, at the same time taking the attitude in which pugilists are usually depicted. "Well, I kin give youse all of dat yer wants; see!"

Nothing was further from Dick's thought than to engage in a fight with the bully, but Bulldog interpreted matters his own way. All Dick cared about was to escape.

Once more the coward hit him, and then Dick's natural courage arose. He would not submit tamely to being beaten, and, with a wild desire in his heart to hit back, his fist shot out.

It would be hard to say who was the more surprised, Dick or the bully, at the effect of the blow. It caught Bulldog on the cheek and forced him back slightly. But it had the effect of further enraging him, and the bully advanced to the attack with an angry look in his eyes.

Suddenly Bulldog's fist shot out, and the blow taking Dick squarely on the chest, sent him reeling and stumbling back. An instant later he fell to the floor. Then the bully sprang forward, all his meaner fighting instincts aroused, determined to cruelly punish the lad, who, he believed, was trying to deceive him.

But at this juncture there was a sound in the hallway outside the door. It was a hurried rush of feet, and some one turned the handle of the door.

"Hey, Bulldog! If you're in there let me in before I bust in the door!" exclaimed a voice.

The bully paused, much surprised.

"Git on away from dere!" he cried.

"Let me in!" insisted the voice.

"Yah! Let us in or ve comes in anyvays," added another.

"It's Dutchy!" said Bulldog, in a whisper.

There came a kick on the rickety old door that made it shake.

"Come on! Open this door. I know you've got Dick in there!" was the demand.

"Git away from dere. Dere's nobody here but me, an' I'll punch yer head if youse don't stop bodderin' me," threatened the bully.

"Jimmy! Jimmy! Here I am! I'm in here!" shouted Dick, rising to his feet and running toward the door.

"Git back dere!" ordered Bulldog, making a grab for Dick as the boy passed him.

But before Dick could reach the door it was burst open from outside, and, tumbling into the room, came Jimmy and Sam, all out of breath from running. Bulldog started back and doubled up his fists. Jimmy made straight for Dick.

"Are you all right? Are you hurt?" he asked anxiously.

"Not—not much. I'm all right."

"He hit you!" exclaimed Jimmy, as he saw a red mark on Dick's face.

"Yes, twice."

"The brute! I'll make him pay for that!"

Jimmy was mad enough now to tackle Bulldog single-handed. But there was no need for this. Sam Schmidt's fighting blood was up. He regarded Jimmy and Dick as his best friends, and the thought that one of them had suffered at the hands of Bulldog made him angry. Sam was a big lad—taller, stronger, and heavier than the bully—but he had no training in fist-fights.

Still he did not hesitate. Straight at Bulldog he leaped, clasping him in his big arms before the bully could strike out, and an instant later the two went down, Bulldog underneath, while Sam rained blow after blow on him.

"So! Dot's de vay I do him," he explained between the thumps. "Next times you vos took somebodies yer own sizes, maybe so. Eh? Dere, dot's fer goot luck," and, with a parting blow, he allowed Bulldog to get up. The bully lost no time in beating a hasty retreat.

Then, for fear he might get some of his cronies and renew the fight, Jimmy advised that they leave, which they did, soon arriving at the lodging-house.

Dick told his story, how he had been enticed away by the untruth about Jimmy being hurt, and the latter related his part in the affair.

"We're well out of it," remarked Dick.

"We ought to tell the police," declared Jimmy.

"Vait. I lick Mike Conroy de next times I sees him, alretty," declared Sam. "Dot vos fun, how I did up der Bulldog! I don't guess dey bodders you two any more."

"I guess not either," added Jimmy.

The story of how Jimmy and Sam had "done up" Bulldog, was soon circulated among the newsboys, and it lost nothing in the telling. When Jimmy and Dick went on the street the next day the former was greeted on all sides as "Champion."

"Sam Schmidt did the most," he said, modestly.

"Dat's all right," answered some of his acquaintances. "Youse is de foist one t' stand out agin Bulldog, an' we're glad of it. Maybe he'll let us alone now." For Bulldog was a terror to the smaller boys.

"I done it for me—I mean my partner," explained Jimmy, with a fond look at Dick. "Anybody what picks on him has to answer to me."

"Dot's right, und I helps, too," added Sam. "Me und Jimmy ve fights togedder, don't ve alretty yet, Jimmy?"

"Sure," replied the hero of the occasion.

It was hot that day, so hot, in fact, that it was hard work to tramp about the streets to sell papers.

"It's me for a dip down at the Battery swimmin' pool when we get through here," remarked Jimmy, as he met his partner at one of the delivery wagons.

"That would be a good idea," said Dick. "I'll go with you."

"I uster go in the fountain basin at City Hall Park," went on Jimmy. "A dip there'd cool a feller off."

"Why don't you now?"

"Cops watches it too close. Some of the fellers goes in, though, but they're likely to lose their clothes. Cops grabs 'em every chance they gits."

The partners separated, Dick to go down to the Wall Street district, and Jimmy to his regular corner. During the afternoon, when Dick sold out, and was about to go for more papers, he was called into a hallway by a broker, who was one of his customers.

"Are you very busy?" the man asked Dick.

"Not so very, sir, just now. I've just sold out, and I need more papers. Why?"

"Well, I'd like you to go on a little errand for me. I want you to take this note over to a firm of brokers," and he named one of the most prominent ones in the financial section. Dick wondered why the man selected him, when there were plenty of messengers he could call by touching a button in his office. The man must have seen the unspoken query on Dick's face, for he said:

"I want you to go, because this is a very important matter, involving a stock deal, and if I send a regular messenger from my office, some other dealers will be sure to notice it, and it may make trouble. You can go without being suspected. Here is the note, and here is a dollar for delivering it."

"That's too much," said Dick quickly.

"I think not," replied the broker with a smile. "You are doing me more of a service than you know. Now don't lose any time."

Dick started off, with the note in his hand.

"Hold on!" called the man quickly. "Don't go out with it that way. Some one may have seen me speaking to you, and suspect something. We have to be very particular down here in Wall Street."

Dick had been down in that section long enough to understand that often the winning or losing of a big financial deal depended on a small matter, such as the broker had mentioned.

"Here, this will be a good way," went on the man, pulling a newspaper from his pocket. "Slip the letter in there, and then, if any one sees you, they'll think you are merely going into the office where I am sending you, to deliver a paper."

Dick did as requested, and was soon on his way, hardly able to believe that he had earned a dollar so easily. He hurried to the office, left his message, without being observed, as far as he could tell, and then he decided he would take a walk up to Barclay Street and see Jimmy.

"I promised him I'd meet him down at the bathhouse," said Dick to himself, "but I don't feel like it. Guess I must be a little under the weather. I don't believe it would be good to go swimming in that water. I'll use the bath-tub at the lodging house."

He went through City Hall Park, on his way to see his partner, for he had emerged in front of the World Building. As he crossed the open space, and approached the fountain, he was aware that something was going on. There was a big crowd about the water basin.

"Maybe somebody's hurt," thought Dick, hastening his steps, but, when he managed to wiggle through the throng, and was close to the edge of the basin, he saw that it was merely the sight of some lads in the fountain that had attracted the crowd.

The hot lads, braving the wrath of the police, of whom none were then present, had taken off all the garments they dared, and had plunged into the cooling water. They were splashing about like birds, enjoying a bath.

The crowd, which always assembles when this scene occurs in the park, was looking on with huge enjoyment, staid business men and millionaire merchants gathering to watch the boys at their sport. The lads splashed and ducked each other, at times, in their eagerness, even wetting the by-standers.

Suddenly there was that cry which, above all others, startles the newsboys and bootblacks of New York.

"Cheese it, de cop!"

Some lookout, posted for that very purpose, had spied the approach of the bluecoat, who came up on the run, seeing the crowd, for he knew what it meant—that the boys were disobeying a city ordinance, and bathing in the basin.

Instantly there was a rush on the part of the lads to get out, for to be caught meant to be arrested and fined. The boys sprang over the side of the basin, the crowd, laughing more heartily than ever, opening to let them escape.

As luck would have it, two or three of the larger boys, in their efforts to get away, ran toward the side of the fountain where Dick stood. He tried to get out of their path, that he might not hamper them in their escape, but there was a fat man behind him and Dick stepped on his toes.

"Ouch! My gracious! That's my corn!" cried the man, limping away.

Dick started to apologize, but he had hardly begun it, when he was fairly overwhelmed by the lads leaping from the basin. They did not care where they landed, as long as they got away from the officer, and they toppled on Dick, splashing water on him from the fountain, and from their own dripping forms.

Dick was knocked down, and one of the boys fell on top of him, the glittering drops splashing all about. Dick struggled to his feet, trying to get rid of the water in his eyes that he might see which way to go to run so as to get out of the way. But, just as he turned to go, he felt some one seize him, and a voice exclaimed:

"Now I've got you, anyhow! Come along with me!"

"Where to? What for?" asked Dick, and he looked up to see that a policeman had him by the shoulder.

"Where to? Why, the station house, of course. And what for? I guess you don't have to ask that! I'll catch some more of you chaps for takin' a dip in the basin the first chance I get, too! You got ahead of me to-day."

"I wasn't in the basin," declared Dick.

"You wasn't? Say, what ye givin' me? Didn't I see ye runnin', an' ain't ye all wet?"

"The water was splashed on me," asserted Dick. "I was just watching them, and some of the boys jumped on me."

"Think I'll believe such a fishy yarn as that?" asked the officer, incredulously. "I seen ye in swimmin', an' ye'll have t' come with me."

"But I wasn't in," insisted Dick, wishing Jimmy was now at hand to aid him.

"Ain't I got eyes in my head?" asked the officer in contempt. "You can't lie out of it that way. Why, you're drippin' wet. You must have gone in with all yer clothes on."

"I didn't go in at all."

"Aw, cut that out an' come along."

Dick did not know what to do. He looked around at the faces of the crowd that had gathered, hoping to see some one to whom he could appeal. But he saw no one. The officer was about to lead him away. All at once a man stepped forth from the throng. He was limping slightly.

"What's he done, officer?" he asked.

The man looked like an influential citizen, and the policeman decided it would be the best policy to answer him.

"Swimmin' in the basin," he said. "Against the law."

"I wasn't in," declared Dick, with tears of mortification in his eyes. "They splashed the water on me. Why, I was standing near you," he went on, for he recognized the man as the fat person, on whose toes he had accidentally stepped.

"Why, bless my soul, so you were!" exclaimed the fleshy gentleman. "Officer, you are making a mistake."

"I guess I know my business," replied the bluecoat shortly. "Move on here. Let me pass or I'll run some of ye in."

"I tell you that you are making a mistake, officer," insisted the fat man, firmly. "This boy stood right in front of me when I was watching the lads in bathing. He was not in the water at all. Why, you can see that for yourself. His shoes are not wet."

Sure enough, though Dick was pretty well soaked all over, his feet had escaped the drenching.

"How do you know he stood in front of you?" inquired the policeman, not accepting the more apparent evidence of the shoes.

"How do I know? The very best reason in the world. He stepped back to get out of the way of the rushing lads, and he came down on my favorite corn. I'm limping yet."

"I'm very sorry," began Dick, who had not had time to finish his apology.

"That's all right," answered the fat man, good-naturedly. "I'll forgive you, and do you a favor in the bargain. No, officer," he went on, "you are mistaken. This boy was not in bathing. I will testify in his favor. Here is my card, if you insist on making an arrest."

He passed a bit of pasteboard over to the policeman, who, when he had read it, took on a different attitude.

"Oh, very well, Alderman Casey," he said, "I beg your pardon. I didn't know he was a friend of yours, or I wouldn't have bothered him. Of course I must have made a mistake. He can go."

"I don't know whether he's a friend of mine or not," continued the alderman with a smile. "I'm inclined to think, by the way my corn hurts, that he isn't. But I want to see justice done. There, my lad, run along now, before you get any wetter, or step on any more fat men's toes," and the alderman, satisfied at having done a good act, and at demonstrating his influence over the police before a crowd, laughed heartily.

Dick lost no time in making his escape, fearing the officer might change his mind. He found Jimmy and related what had occurred.

"Crimps! Say, you has luck!" exclaimed Dick's partner. "Alderman Casey is one of the big-bugs! What, didn't you know him when he was speakin' to youse—I mean you?"

"No."

"Well, of course it takes time to know all the main gazabos of this town," spoke Jimmy, with an air of lofty wisdom. "But I'm sorry you don't feel well. Come an' have a soda."

"No, I don't think I care for any. I don't believe it would be good for me. But you go get one."

"All right, I will. Then you won't come swimmin' to-night, Dick?"

"No, I've had enough of it for one day. I guess I'll be better in the morning."

Dick did not feel very well that night when he went to bed. The excitement had a bad effect on his nerves, and when he awoke in the morning, he had quite a fever. His face was flushed and his breathing rapid. He tried to get up to go out with his papers, but found himself too dizzy to stand.

"I—I guess I'm sick, Jimmy," he said. "But I'll be all right in a little while. You go ahead out, so as not to lose the morning trade."

"What? And leave you here all alone, and sick? I guess not much! Wait, I'll call Mr. Snowden. He knows somethin' about medicine."

CHAPTER XXI

JIMMY IN TROUBLE

When the manager of the lodging-house saw Dick, he realized that the lad was quite ill. He did not try to prescribe for him, but at once called in the district physician.

The doctor looked grave when he had felt of Dick's pulse, looked at his tongue, and asked him some questions. Then he beckoned Mr. Snowden to come out of the room.

"What is it?" asked the manager.

"I'm afraid the lad's going to be quite ill. I can't be positive, but I don't like his symptoms. He must have had some shock recently that brought this on. He looks like a boy from some refined home. How does he come to be in this place?" This physician was not the one who had seen Dick before.

Mr. Snowden explained as much about Dick's case as he knew, ending up with an account of Bulldog's meanness.

"That fright was what brought it on," declared the doctor. "Well, I'll leave some medicine for him, and I'll come in again this afternoon. He ought to have some one to look after him."

"I guess we can arrange that. His 'partner,' as he calls him, Jimmy Small, is very kind to him. The two boys have done well selling papers, and I understand they have quite a tidy little sum saved up. They are trying to buy a stand. I guess Jimmy will stay in and look after him, and I will do what I can."

"Perhaps that will answer. He may take a turn for the better. I can tell in a few hours."

Mr. Snowden had a talk with Jimmy, telling him part of what the doctor had said, but not enough to alarm the lad. As he expected, Jimmy at once offered to stay at home and nurse Dick, as he had done once before.

"But what about selling the papers?" asked the manager.

"I can get Sam Schmidt and Frank Merton to look after part of my customers for me. The rest will have to wait until Dick gets well."

This arrangement was carried out, Frank and Sam gladly agreeing to do all in their power to help the two boys. Dick was quite ill, but fortunately nothing very serious developed. His fever still continued, however, and he was too weak to get out of bed, the physician said.

"How long will I have to stay in?" asked Dick.

"At least a week. Perhaps longer. You require nourishing food, and your nerves need quieting. You are not used to this life."

"No," said Dick softly, and again there came to him the troublesome question of what sort a life he was accustomed to, and who he was.

"But you must not worry," cautioned the doctor. "You'll be well taken care of, and in a short time you can go out again."

In a few days Dick was enough better so that he did not need any one with him constantly. Jimmy, therefore, could go out on the streets selling papers, for Mr. Snowden or some of the men employed about the lodging-house looked in Dick's room several times during the day to see if he needed anything.

"Lots of men is askin' for you," said Jimmy, when he came home one night. "Sam Schmidt is takin' care of your customers down in Wall Street, and they want to know when you're comin' back. They say they're waitin' for you, and for a while they'll buy of Sam. He tried to explain that he was workin' for you, but he can't twist his Dutch tongue well enough yet. But I guess it's all right."

Dick did not recover as quickly as the doctor expected he would, and he had been in bed over a week, for the fever did not seem to yield to the treatment.

"It must be some trouble that I can't get at," said the baffled physician one day to Mr. Snowden. "Perhaps that blow he got just before he found himself in the box may have had something to do with it. If he doesn't get better soon I'll have him taken to the hospital. We may have to operate."

"Don't tell him or Jimmy that."

"Oh, no; not until it's necessary. I'll try some new medicine."

It was the day following this that something happened which changed everything, and while at the time it seemed to Jimmy quite a misfortune, in the end it turned into a blessing.

As might be expected, Mike Conroy and Bulldog Smouder were much incensed at the failure of their plot. Jimmy had reached New York much quicker than they had thought he would, thanks to the kindness of the woman who supplied him with carfare, and to whom, with Dick's help that same night, he had mailed back the twenty-five cents with a letter of thanks. Then, too, Sam's unexpected aid and his beating of Bulldog made that bully very angry. So the two cronies were looking for a chance to get "even," as they called it.

They had about given up trying to get any reward for restoring Dick to his home, and they began to believe that the boy was telling the truth about himself. But their anger turned against Jimmy, whom they both regarded as their enemy. They were on the lookout for an opportunity to injure him in some way.

Chance gave them the very opportunity they wanted. It was in the afternoon, Jimmy was selling the last of his papers, and was counting on getting back to the room where Dick was. An Italian banana peddler stopped his cart right behind the boy and began to arrange the fruit in tempting piles. Just then Bulldog and Mike passed, and as Jimmy was counting his change he did not see them.

"Shove him over inter de Ginny's cart an' run," suggested Mike.

"Sure," agreed his crony, always ready for a mean trick.

When Jimmy was not looking Mike stepped quickly up and gave the newsboy a vigorous push. Jimmy lost his balance, and the next instant was fairly on top of the cart. It upset, and he rolled to the ground amid bunches of the yellow fruit.

"Comme sta!" wildly exclaimed the Italian. "Whatta for you doa dat? Badda de boy! Me calla de police! Upseta alla de banan!"

"I didn't do it. They pushed me," said Jimmy as he struggled to his feet and started to point out Bulldog and Mike, of whom he had caught a passing glimpse as they fled. But they had hid in a doorway and could not be seen.

"Nobody doa de push!" declared the Italian. "Badda de boya, makea me mucha de troub! Hey, police!" and he beckoned to a big bluecoat.

"Now what's the row?" asked the officer.

"Dessa boy he upseta my stand. Spoila alla de banan."

"I didn't do it," declared Jimmy.

"Aw, g'wan! Didn't I see you on top of the cart," said the officer. There had recently been a concerted protest on the part of Italian peddlers against newsboys and bootblacks who annoyed them, and as the Italian vote was getting large, interested politicians had induced the police captains to instruct their men to be on the lookout to arrest boys who bothered the peddlers. So the officer took more interest in this case than otherwise he would have done.

"Some one pushed me," asserted Jimmy again.

"That's a likely story. I seen you do it. Now I'm goin' to run you in," and with that the bluecoat arrested Jimmy and marched him off to the police station, the Italian following with his cart to make a complaint.

CHAPTER XXII

MR. CROSSCRAB IS ROBBED

Jimmy was in despair. He did not see how he was going to convince the sergeant in the station-house that he was innocent of the charge. Certainly to the policeman and the Italian it did look as if Jimmy had deliberately jumped on the cart, thus upsetting it.

And another matter worried Jimmy. He knew that if the stories of the policeman and peddler were believed he would probably be locked up over night for a hearing before the magistrate the next morning. Meanwhile who would look after Dick?

"Crimps! but this is bad luck!" thought Jimmy. "If I only had some one to go my bail maybe I could get off."

But he could think of no one on whom he might call. Jimmy's acquaintance was not among those capable of signing bail bonds.

A big crowd had gathered when the arrest was made, and Jimmy looked in vain among the throng for some friendly person by whom he could send word to Mr. Snowden of his plight He thought the manager might be able to help him.

Then when the officer led him away quite a number of newsboys and bootblacks followed. Reaching the precinct station-house, Jimmy was taken inside and made to stand in front of the big brass railing surrounding the desk, while the sergeant prepared to hear what the policeman had to say.

"Here's a kid that upset the Italian's cart," explained the bluecoat. "I seen him do it."

"Dat's a'right, Mr. Police," added the peddler. "He badda de boy. Knocka alla de banan in de streeta."

"What's your name?" asked the sergeant, drawing the blotter, or slate, toward him. On this were written the names of prisoners, and Jimmy, who had often been in station-houses when men were locked up, knew what was coming next.

"You're not going to lock me up, are you?" he asked.

"That's what we are," replied the sergeant. "This business of annoying the Italians has got to stop." He was only carrying out the orders of his superiors.

"But I didn't do it."

"Well, you can prove that to the judge in the morning and he'll let you go."

"Sure he done it," repeated the policeman. "I seen him."

Which was true enough as far as it went. The officer was honestly mistaken, as was the Italian. The sergeant wrote down Jimmy's name and other information which the lad gave.

"Anybody go your bail?" and the sergeant looked up on asking the usual question, for in such minor offenses as this he was empowered to take bail for prisoners.

"If you could send to Mr. Snowden, manager of the Newsboys' Lodging House, I'm sure he would," said Jimmy.

"Got any money to pay for a messenger?"

"Sure," and the newsboy hauled out a handful of change.

"All right," remarked the sergeant indifferently. "Doorman, lock him up and then call a messenger for him."

Even though he was to be locked in a cell, Jimmy did not mind it so much, now that there was a chance to get word to Mr. Snowden. He was searched, his money being all that was returned to him, his knife and some other possessions being retained by the sergeant until he should be bailed or discharged. Then the doorman summoned a district messenger boy, to whom Jimmy talked through the bars of his cell, instructing him to inform Mr. Snowden what had happened and ask him to come to the police-station.

Meanwhile the policeman had gone back on his beat, and the Italian, having been instructed to appear at court in the morning, was allowed to go. He had left his cart in front of the station-house, and his stock of bananas was much less when he came out, as the temptation of the fruit had been too much for the crowd of boys.

Mr. Snowden came promptly in response to Jimmy's request, and soon arranged for bail for the lad. So a few hours after he was arrested Jimmy was free again, but he would have to be tried in the morning.

"I'd advise you," said the sergeant, who took more interest in Jimmy's case when he heard from the lodging-house superintendent what sort of a lad the newsboy was, "to hunt up these two chaps you say pushed you. If you see them call a policeman and have them arrested. You can make a charge against them."

"But will a cop—I mean a policeman—arrest them on my say-so?" asked Jimmy.

"I guess so. Wait, I'll give you a note, and you can show it to the officer nearest at hand when you see those two chaps," and the sergeant wrote out a note for Jimmy.

Then with Mr. Snowden the boy left the station-house, his mind made up to search for Mike and Bulldog and cause their arrest. And this was not so much because he was vindictive as that he wanted to be cleared of the unjust charge.

"How's Dick?" asked Jimmy of the lodging-house manager.

"Not quite so well," was the grave answer. "But don't worry. I guess he'll be all right."

"I suppose I'd better go back and take care of him instead of chasing after Mike and Bulldog."

"No, perhaps it will be well for you to stay away. He will be sure to question you, and if he hears of your arrest it might excite him. I will tell him you are all right, but that you have some business to attend to. Meanwhile you can look for those two young rowdies. I hope you find them. I'll look out for Dick; so don't worry."

After a hasty supper Jimmy set out to find the two bullies, with the note from the sergeant safe in his pocket. He knew where Mike and Bulldog usually were to be found at night—in the neighborhood of some of the moving picture shows—and thither Jimmy went.

As he walked down the Bowery he saw a crowd in front of a brilliantly-lighted store, the proprietor of which, to draw trade, had installed a small cage of monkeys. There was quite a throng of men and boys watching the antics of the creatures.

As Jimmy approached the outer line of people he saw, standing close together near the window, the two bullies whom he sought. This was unexpected good luck, and he looked around for a policeman. He saw one not far off, and then seeing a newsboy whom he knew, Jimmy quietly whispered to the latter to summon the officer.

"What fer?" asked the lad.

"You'll see in a minute. There's going to be some fun."

For Jimmy had made up his mind to grab both the bullies and hold them until the officer could arrive, regardless of what they might do to him, though he knew they would beat and kick him in an endeavor to get away. But he calculated it could not last long, as just before he prepared to tackle the two he saw the officer start toward the throng.

"Now for it," said Jimmy in a whisper to himself.

But just then something most unexpected happened. As Jimmy crept closer to the two unsuspecting ones he saw the hand of Mike Conroy slip into the pocket of a man standing near him. Softly and slowly the hand was inserted, and a moment later it was withdrawn, holding a pocketbook.

"He's picking that man's pocket!" thought Jimmy. "Now I can make another charge against him."

He made a sudden grab for Mike. At the same instant the man who had been robbed turned around, for he felt some movement in his pocket.

"Mr. Crosscrab!" exclaimed Jimmy, as he saw the man's face.

"Why, Jimmy, I've been looking for you!" cried the young man. "But what's this? My pocketbook!"

For he saw it in Mike's hand, which Jimmy held in a firm grasp.

"He stole it!" cried Jimmy.

"I did not! I found it on de sidewalk, an' I were jest goin' t' hand it back t' him!" cried the bully.

"Hold him, Mr. Crosscrab!" cried Jimmy, making a grab for Bulldog, who, seeing how matters were going, was trying to sneak away. Mr. Crosscrab acted promptly, and Mike struggled in vain to get loose.

"Let me go or I'll smash youse a good one!" threatened Bulldog, but Jimmy held grimly on.

"What's the row?" asked the policeman, hurrying through the crowd that had encircled the four.

"He tried to rob me," explained Mr. Crosscrab, and it was very evident, for the pocketbook had fallen to the sidewalk when Mike opened his hand.

"All right. I'll take him in. You'll have to come along and make a charge."

"I'll do it."

"And I want this one arrested!" exclaimed Jimmy.

"What for?" and the officer looked surprised. "Are there two of 'em?"

"This fellow upset an Italian's cart by pushing me into it to-day," explained Jimmy, keeping hold of Bulldog despite the latter's efforts to get away. "I was arrested for it, and the sergeant said I should have him and Mike locked up as witnesses. Here's a note," and with much difficulty Jimmy took it out and handed it to the policeman.

"I didn't do it. It was Mike," declared Bulldog.

"Youse done it yerself," said Mike.

The policeman quickly read the note. Meanwhile Mr. Crosscrab had been holding Mike, and the crowd was now so thick that Bulldog had no chance to escape, even if he had dared risk it with an officer at hand.

"All right. I'll lock 'em both up," said the officer, taking one arm of each of the prisoners. "Make way there. I'll ring for the wagon."

"I'll do it for you," volunteered Jimmy, for he had once opened a patrol box and sent in a call for a policeman who had his hands full with a refractory prisoner.

"All right. You're a smart kid. Here's my key," and the bluecoat passed it over, temporarily letting go of Mike, but grabbing him again as the thief started to run.

Meanwhile Mr. Crosscrab had picked up his pocketbook, and with Jimmy followed the officer and his two prisoners, while the crowd trailed along in the rear. The patrol box was soon reached and Jimmy sent in the call. In a few minutes the wagon arrived, and Mike and Bulldog, both protesting their innocence, were taken to the station-house.

CHAPTER XXIII

BACK AT BUSINESS

Formalities at the police-station were soon complied with. Mr. Crosscrab made a complaint of robbery against Mike Conroy, and that bully was locked up. There was also Jimmy's charge against him, and in this was also included Bulldog, so that youth, too, was put into a cell. Mr. Crosscrab and Jimmy were told to appear in the morning as witnesses.

"Well, Jimmy," remarked Mr. Crosscrab when they were in the street once more, "you seem to be right on hand when you're wanted."

"It was mostly luck that I prevented him from robbing you though. But I did myself a good turn, for now I can be cleared of the charge of upsetting the banana cart."

"If my pocketbook had been stolen it would have meant a serious loss to me."

"How so?"

"It contains a large sum of money. I am going back to my home in Newton, Vermont, to-morrow, and I have to take quite a sum with me to conclude some business matters in which I am engaged. So if Mike had gotten away with the cash I would have been put to considerable loss."

"Then I am glad I saw him in time. When are you coming around to see me and my partner, Mr. Crosscrab? He's sick."

"I am sorry to hear that. I meant to come before this, but I have been quite busy since coming to New York. Then my aunt being taken ill made me change my plans. However, she is better now, and that is why I am going home."

"Are you coming back to New York?"

"Yes, I expect to return in about a week, and then I will be glad to call and see you. I hope Dick Box will soon be better. I never can help thinking what a queer name that is."

"It is rather odd, but we can't seem to get a better one for him nor discover his real one."

"That is too bad. I would like very much to see him, and I will just as soon as I get back. I would call to-night, only it is getting late and I have several matters to attend to. But I will see you at court in the morning."

Jimmy bade his friend good-night and hurried to the lodging-house, for he was anxious about Dick. However, he found his partner much better, and the doctor said he thought the boy would now speedily recover as his fever had entirely left him.

Mike and Bulldog were given a preliminary hearing the next day. On the charge of theft Mike was remanded in heavy bail for the Grand Jury's action, and Bulldog was also held as a witness. Then Jimmy was arraigned on the charge, made by the policeman, that he had tipped over the Italian's cart.

But the previous complaints against the two youths had their effect on Jimmy's case. He told his story, saying how Bulldog and Mike had pushed him, and the Italian, who had calmed down to a considerable extent, gave such testimony that it convinced the magistrate Jimmy was telling the truth. Mike and Bulldog were questioned, and finally had to admit that they were the guilty ones.

So they were convicted on that charge, and were sentenced to pay a fine of ten dollars each. As they did not have the money, and could not get bail on the other charge, they were taken to the Tombs prison, while Jimmy was allowed to go. Incidentally the magistrate complimented Jimmy on the manner in which he had caused the arrest of the two young criminals.

"Well, I suppose I will have to appear later when Mike's regular trial comes off," remarked Mr. Crosscrab as he parted from Jimmy in front of the police court. "But that will not be for some time. Now I am off for Vermont, but I will not forget to see you when I return. Give my regards to your partner, in whom, though I have never seen him, I take a great deal of interest. Poor Dick Box; I must help you to find a better name for him when I get back."

"I wish you would. The police can't seem to help him."

"Then I will. Good-by, Jimmy."

"Good-by, Mr. Crosscrab."

Jimmy started back to work with a lighter heart than he had had in many a day, and the principal cause of it was that Dick was getting better. He would be able to be out in a few days, the doctor said.

So Jimmy hustled around and sold a large number of papers. Frank Merton and Sam Schmidt had been helping the partners, and business had not been so bad, though of course the profits were largely taken up in paying the two boys who did Dick's work.

One afternoon, at the close of the day's business, Sam Schmidt came to Jimmy with every appearance of excitement.

"What's the matter, Sam?" asked Jimmy. "Found a pocketbook full of bills?"

"Nope, but I haf alretty found somedings else."

"What is it?"

"I haf found der advertisement about dot Box feller."

"What! About Dick? Have you found something about him in the paper?" for Sam had not given up looking for a notice in the personal columns of the papers, which might refer to the strange new boy who had come into the midst of the news-lads.

"For sure, I haf. Here it iss," and Sam pulled out a piece torn from the Herald.

"Read it," said Jimmy. "I ain't quite quick enough on me—I mean my—words yet. You read it."

"Vell, I am not so good on der Englishness of it, but dis is vot it means. 'If der boy vot runned avay from his home vill come back all vill be forgiveness, und der money he took to go und fight der Indians mit, he can keep, for his mudder und his fadder is sorrowfulness mitout him, und vould he please write or sends a message und all vill be vell, und he kin haf der pony und der bicycle vot he wants.' Dot's all dere is to it."

"But don't it say who he is—who the kid is?—though I don't believe it's Dick that's meant."

"Sure it says who it is vot put it in der paper," replied Sam. "It says dot der boy is to address Mr. Samuel Wonsonski, New York City."

"Then it ain't Dick," decided Jimmy.

"Vy not? Ain't it got referenceness to a boy vot runned avay; und ain't Dick a runavay?"

"I don't know as he is. Anyhow, this can't be about him."

"Vy not?"

"Because this is the name of either a Jew or a Russian, and Dick's an American."

"Oh, maybe dot's so," agreed Sam. "But you can't always sometimes tell. Maybe he is a part Jew and part Russian and part American. Ve had better ask him, I dinks."

"Well, it wouldn't do any harm, I s'pose," admitted Jimmy. "Come ahead over to the lodging-house, and we'll tell him about this advertisement."

They found Dick feeling pretty comfortable, and, as he seemed able to converse about the mystery, Jimmy began on the subject that had brought Sam and himself to his partner's room.

"Dick," asked Jimmy, "you don't s'pose you ran away to fight Indians; did you?"

"Fight Indians? No. Why?"

"And you didn't take any money from your dad; did you?"

"Of course not. What makes you ask such questions?"

"Because it's in der paper," replied Sam. "See, iss dis got anyding to do mit you?" and he held out the torn piece of the newspaper.

Dick read it quickly, and slowly shook his head. A look of hope had come into his face when Sam had extended the slip, but it faded away again, leaving him pale and wan.

"No, I'm sure that isn't my name," he said.

"Are you sure?" asked Sam, who hated to give up the idea.

"Very sure."

"But didn't you want a pony?" asked the German youth.

"No, as near as I can remember, I had a horse or a pony," replied Dick. "I seem to recall something about owning one. I know I used to take long drives in a carriage, through a beautiful country."

"Den you didn't lif in New York," declared Sam, positively. "Dis is a great city, but dere ain't no beautiful country about it. I know. I lived in der country in der Vaterland, und dot vos country dere vot *vos* country," and he sighed in regret.

He looked at the piece of paper once more.

"Vait!" he exclaimed. "Vos you ever haf a desire for a bicycle? Maybe dot's it. Maybe your fadder vouldn't gif you a bicycle, und you runned avay to hund Indians, und dey scalped you, und took your remembery mit 'em."

"Oh, no, no!" exclaimed Dick, laughing in spite of himself. "I never cared much for a bicycle. I'm sure I shouldn't have run away from home because I couldn't have one."

"Und der Indians didn't scalp you?" asked Sam, as if still in doubt.

"No, indeed. I've got all my hair yet, even if my memory has gone back on me. I guess that must refer to some other boy. Why, of course it does. Here it says his first name is Isaac, and the description isn't at all like me."

"Vell, dot's so," admitted Sam, when he had read the item over again. "I guess it must be somebodies else dan you. I'm sorry, Dick. I thought sure I hat found out who you vos."

"I wish you had, Sam, but I'll find out some day."

Dick sighed in regret, for the strain was beginning to tell on him. Nevertheless he bore up well.

At the end of the week Dick was able to go out, and he felt so well that he insisted that he be allowed to sell papers.

"I don't think you're able to," objected Jimmy.

"Oh, yes, I am. Besides, I want to earn some money. I've been quite an expense to you."

"Crimps! I don't mean that. But that's nothing. Look what you did for me. I'm ever so much better off since I met you."

"I am glad you think so, but you must have had to draw some of our savings out of the bank for medicine and things, and I want to put it back so we can purchase that stand before Christmas, if possible."

"Oh, Christmas is quite a ways off. Besides, I only used about five dollars from the bank. Business has been very good lately, even with paying Frank and Sam a commission."

Since Dick's illness Jimmy had developed quite a business talent, and as he could now read and write some, he attended to matters connected with their little bank account, putting some in and at times drawing a dollar or so out, as it was needed.

Though Jimmy insisted that Dick take a rest before beginning to sell papers, the latter would not hear of it. The next day he started out with his bundle as usual, glad to be back at business once more. He was welcomed by many of his former customers, who remembered him, and he sold a large number of papers.

"How do you feel?" asked Jimmy that night when the partners were in their room.

"Pretty good, only a little tired. My, what a lot has happened since that night I thought you were hurt!"

"I should say so. Mike and Bulldog will not bother us for quite a while, I guess," and this proved a correct surmise, for some time later, at the trial, they were both convicted and sent to a reform school for long terms. Jimmy never recovered the money which Mike stole from him at the moving picture show nor that taken in Brooklyn.

"Yes, lots of things happened," went on Dick, "only I wish a little more had."

"What do you mean?"

"I mean I wish I knew who I was."

Jimmy said nothing. He did not like to see Dick sad, but he did not know how to help him in this matter. Would the mystery never be solved?

CHAPTER XXIV

MR. CROSSCRAB'S VISIT

Business with the partners went on as usual for several days. There was a brisk demand for papers, and slowly they saw the little savings in the bank grow. They began to have visions of a fine stand by Christmas, and the one they had first considered was still in their mind, for the owner had not succeeded in disposing of it.

"Dick," remarked Jimmy one night, "I've got a new scheme."

"What is it?" and Dick looked up from the book he was reading at his partner on the other side of the table. Jimmy was laboriously figuring on the back of an old envelope.

"Well, you know that weekly illustrated paper that's making such a hit now? It comes out every Friday, an' lots of the boys sell it."

"Yes, I know the one you mean. What about it?"

"I was thinking we might add it to our stock. If we did, and sold enough of 'em, we could make quite a bit. There's two and a half cents profit on each copy, and if we sold fifty each that'd be two dollars and a half each week."

"Good! You're coming on with your arithmetic," exclaimed Dick. "Why, that sounds good, Jimmy. Let's do it."

"There's one thing agin it, though."

"What's that?"

"There's no returns. You can't take back what you don't sell, and we might lose on it."

"Well, I suppose we'll have to take that risk. Business men generally have to venture something."

"I know, but we ain't got much capital. If we was to lose a dollar in the week it wouldn't be no fun."

"No; still I think it's worth trying."

"Then I'll do it. I'll order a stock for this Friday, and we'll see what we can do."

Jimmy was glad his chum had agreed to the scheme, which the older newsboy had had in mind for some time, ever since he saw how well some of his companions were doing with the new weekly, which was making quite a bid for trade.

Accordingly, when Friday came, Jimmy got up early, and purchased one hundred copies of the periodical. These he divided with Dick, and the two boys, rather more heavily laden than usual, started out for their day's business.

If Dick thought he was going to dispose of all his copies of the new weekly quickly, he was much disappointed. Down in the financial section he sold his usual number of daily papers, but, when it came to disposing of the other, he had no luck.

"Why, I get that magazine at home every Friday morning," said one broker, the one for whom Dick had delivered the letter that day he nearly was arrested at the park fountain. "I subscribe for it."

"Then you don't want two copies," spoke Dick cheerfully, though he began to have his doubts about Jimmy's new scheme.

He found that nearly every person whom he asked to buy the weekly received it at his house, either through the mail, or from some boy who had a route in that vicinity. He did manage to sell a few copies, but not enough to pay for carrying the fifty around.

"I don't believe you'll have much of a success with that," said a banker, who was one of Dick's steady customers. "The concern sent out an army of agents to get subscriptions by the year, before allowing boys to sell it on the streets, and persons down here haven't time to read a magazine like that during business hours. We get it at our homes."

Before the day was over Dick began to believe this was true. He only managed to sell twelve copies out of the fifty he had taken out, and, as the sale of the magazine was practically over on the day of publication, he could see a financial loss staring him in the face.

"That is, unless Jimmy managed to dispose of all of his," he thought. "Guess I'll quit now, and go up and see how he's making out."

He found Jimmy on his corner, busily engaged in disposing of the evening papers, for his customers did not stop work as early as did those in the financial section.

"How's the new weekly going, Jimmy?" asked 'Dick, when there came a lull in trade.

"Rotten!" was Jimmy's characteristic answer. "It's a regular lemon, down here. It's on de blink. I sold ten copies, and I couldn't get rid of another one. So I stowed 'em away, and I got busy with me—I mean my—regular papers. No trouble to sell them. How'd you make out?"

"Not much better. I sold twelve."

"Say, ain't that the limit? I'll never try a new stunt like that ag'in. Everybody I struck to buy one, had one already, or got it home."

"Same with me," agreed Dick.

"Well, I can see us losin' some of our hard-earned plunks," went on Jimmy.

"Never mind," consoled his partner. "We made a good try, and we'll know better next time."

"You bet I will. What's that the book says about a trolley conductor stickin' to his car?"

"I guess you mean the one about the shoemaker sticking to his last," said Dick, with a smile.

"Well, last or first, it don't make much difference, only I'm going to stick to daily papers after this. Crimps! T'ink what a lot of fun we could have had with de chink we lost!"

"Well, we'll make it up, somehow," said Dick. "Don't worry over it."

But Jimmy could not help it, and it was some time before he got over the financial disaster which came to him and his partner. However, it was, as Dick said, a good lesson to them, not to venture into a field of which they knew nothing.

Jimmy had, under Dick's guidance, resumed his studies at night, and Frank Merton came in occasionally. The boys began to plan on attending night school as soon as the term opened, which would be in a few weeks.

"Then you'll have to study harder than you do now, Jimmy," said Dick. "Those teachers will not be as easy on you as I am."

"Well, I guess I can stand it," answered Jimmy, with a little sigh. "As long as I've got to read and write and do arithmetic, I might as well learn to do it good."

One evening, when Jimmy had not come in, as he had undertaken to dispose of a lot of late extras, Dick sat alone in the room. He was vainly puzzling over his queer case, and wondering if he would ever learn who he was, and who his folks were, if he had any. He tried and tried again to penetrate back into the past, but he had to stop at a certain place. And that was a confused scene, where he found himself in a crowd, felt a stunning blow on the head and then awoke in the box with Jimmy.

"I'm afraid that's as near it as I ever shall get," thought poor Dick. "If only I could see something, or somebody, or hear something said that would recall the past. But I can't."

A little later some one knocked on the door. Thinking it was Mr. Snowden, who used to call on the permanent lodgers in the house occasionally, Dick called out an invitation to enter.

A tall young man came in. He was a stranger to Dick, who looked at him in the light of the gas-jet, wondering what was wanted.

"Is Jimmy Small here?" asked the young man.

"He is out selling papers," replied Dick. "I'm his partner. Can I do anything for you."

"Well, I just dropped in to pay him a friendly visit, as I promised I would. I'm Mr. Crosscrab."

"Oh, yes, I've often heard Jimmy speak of you. Won't you sit down. He'll soon be in."

Dick stepped out of the shadow cast by a shelf on the wall and offered Mr. Crosscrab a chair. As the light fell upon the boy's face the visitor stepped back in amazement.

"Who—who are you?" asked Mr. Crosscrab.

"Why, I'm Jimmy's partner."

"Yes, but what—what is your name?"

"Well, Jimmy calls me Dick Box. My first name is Dick, but I have forgotten my other."

"Yes, yes! I know. You're Dick Box. At least, that's what Jimmy calls you. But—yes, it must be—yet I had better make certain before I tell him," and these last words Mr. Crosscrab murmured in a low voice.

Dick did not know what to make of the man's manner.

"What is it?" he asked. "What is the matter?"

"I wish I had known this before I went to Vermont," went on Mr. Crosscrab, speaking to himself. "Yet it must be the same one. But how could he be here when he's supposed to be in Chicago?"

Dick began to be a little alarmed. He thought perhaps Mr. Crosscrab might be a little insane. He wished Jimmy would come in.

"Can't you remember your other name?" asked the visitor. "Try—try very hard."

"I have tried—every day, but it's no use."

"Do you know where you came from?"

"No. All I can remember is a large house with lots of ground about it, and a man and woman who were kind to me. Oh, Mr. Crosscrab, do you know anything about me? Do you know who I am? Tell me, please, if you do!"

"I am not sure, yet you look exactly the same. Tell me, can you remember anything about the house where you used to live?"

Dick puzzled his brain. Strange shadows seemed to flit past him, yet they meant nothing.

"Can you recall a little brook that used to run in front of the house, across the road, and a little rustic bridge that spanned it?" asked Mr. Crosscrab.

"Yes! Yes!" cried Dick eagerly. "I begin to remember now. Help me, please do!"

At that instant the door opened and Jimmy entered. He looked in surprise at Mr. Crosscrab, and then Dick's manner showed him something unusual was taking place.

"What is the matter, Dick?" he asked. "Are you sick again?"

"No, but Mr. Crosscrab thinks he knows who I am. He is trying to help me remember."

"I am not sure," replied the visitor in answer to Jimmy's look. "This is the first time I have seen your partner, and I do not want to raise false hopes. Yet he may be a certain boy of whom I heard on my recent visit to my home in Vermont."

"Who is he?" asked Jimmy.

"Perhaps I had better tell you the story," suggested Mr. Crosscrab. "Then we can decide what to do. But don't be disappointed if, after all, the secret of Dick Box is still unsolved."

"Oh, I hope I can find out who I am," murmured the boy who had forgotten the past.

"When I was home this trip," went on Mr. Crosscrab, "I heard my father tell about a friend of his owning a farm not far away whose son is missing. The boy had been gone for several months, but the father only just learned of it."

"How was that?" asked Jimmy.

"This way: The farmer I speak of lived with his wife and son on a big farm near my father's. One day, some time ago, all three started for New York. The farmer and his wife had to go to Europe to settle up an estate to which the farmer had fallen heir, and his wife went with him. As they expected to travel about considerably, for part of the property was in Germany and part in France, they decided not to take their son with them. He was to be sent to a cousin in Chicago who would care for him until his parents returned.

"The three arrived in New York, where the boy was to take a train for Chicago and the father and mother embark on a ship for Europe. They took their son to the Grand Central Station here, and, bidding him farewell, left him just before he was to take his train as they had to go aboard their vessel. That was the last they saw of their son. They went to Europe, and as they had to travel about more than they expected they lost considerable of their mail. They never got a letter from the cousin in Chicago telling about their son, but they did not worry, for, though they would liked to have heard from him, they thought he was all right. They wrote a number of letters to him, but he never got them."

"Why not?" asked Dick, who was deeply interested.

"Because the boy never got to Chicago. He disappeared somewhere between here and there, maybe after arriving in the western city. His father and mother never knew it until they came back from Europe last week. Then, in answer to a telegram to the cousin in Chicago asking how their son was, there came a message saying he had never arrived. The cousin, after receiving letters from the other side, which indicated that the boy's parents believed their son was with her, had tried to send them word that he had never arrived, but of course the messages did not reach the boy's father and mother.

"So they never knew until they got back the other day that he has been missing all this while. They are heartbroken, and they have hired private detectives to find him if possible. This is the story my father told me when I was home, and he showed me a picture of the missing boy."

"Does the picture look like me?" demanded Dick.

"Very much. So much so that I was startled when I came in here and saw you."

"What's the missing boy's name?" asked Jimmy.

"Dick Sanden."

"That's me! That's me!" exclaimed Dick, springing to his feet. "I remember now! I'm Dick Box no longer! I'm Dick Sanden! I remember it all! Oh, how glad I am!"

"Are you sure?" asked Mr. Crosscrab, for he did not want the boy to be mistaken. "Be careful now. What is your father's name?"

"My father's name? My father's name?" murmured Dick. "I—I can't seem to remember." He passed his hand across his forehead. "I can't recall that," he said piteously.

CHAPTER XXV

WHO DICK BOX WAS—CONCLUSION

Crossing the room Mr. Crosscrab put his arm about Dick.

"You must calm yourself," he said, for the boy was on the verge of tears and a nervous breakdown. "Let us reason this matter out. I really believe we can establish your identity, but we must go slowly. Your memory can not all come back at once. It will take a little time."

"Do you know his father's name?" asked Jimmy.

"Yes, if that man is his father. But I wanted to see if he could recall it. That would almost prove that Dick Box is Dick Sanden. Mr. Sanden's name is Oliver, and he lives in the township of Slaterville, Vermont."

"That's it! I remember now!" cried Dick joyfully. "My father is Mr. Oliver Sanden, of Slaterville. Now I am sure who I am."

"We must not be too positive," cautioned Mr. Crosscrab with a smile. "Your memory may be playing you tricks again, and you may think because I mention a name that it is the one you have forgotten. However, we can soon make sure."

"How?" inquired Jimmy with tremendous interest.

"I will telegraph my father to go at once and see Mr. Sanden. He can come here to-morrow morning, and then we can make positive if Dick Box is Richard Sanden."

"I'm sure I am," said Dick with a smile. "It is beginning to come back to me now. I remember father and mother starting for Europe and how I was to go to Chicago."

"What happened after you got to the Grand Central Station?" asked Jimmy. "Why didn't you go to Chicago?"

"That's something I can't remember. That's still a puzzle."

"Well, don't worry over it," advised Mr. Crosscrab. "We will try and have it all straightened out to-morrow. You had better lie down and rest."

"Lie down! I couldn't lie down when I am thinking this way," replied Dick. "I am so anxious to see my parents."

After a few more questions Mr. Crosscrab was reasonably certain that Dick Box was indeed Dick Sanden, for Dick could describe different parts of the farm and things in Slaterville with which Mr. Crosscrab was familiar.

The two boys were eager to talk over the unexpected discovery of Dick's identity as made by Mr. Crosscrab, but the latter insisted that Dick must be kept quiet, and he threatened to take Jimmy away unless they got more calm, as he feared Dick would become ill again.

It seemed to Dick that he would never get to sleep, but at length his brain, tired with the many thoughts that flitted through it, was quiet, and he slept heavily until morning. Meanwhile Mr. Crosscrab had sent off the telegram.

Dick and Jimmy decided not to sell papers the next day. They were both too excited to pay proper attention to the business, and Frank Merton and Sam Schmidt were called on.

How long the hours seemed before it would be possible for Mr. Sanden to arrive! There had come a telegram to Mr. Crosscrab stating that he had started from Slaterville at midnight and expected to be in New York about noon.

As Jimmy, Dick and Mr. Crosscrab sat in the room of the newsboy partners anxiously waiting there sounded out in the corridor the tramp of several feet.

"That's the room right in there," they heard Mr. Snowdon say, directing some one. The next instant the door opened. In rushed a man and woman.

"Dick!" they exclaimed in a breath, and a moment later Dick was folded in the arms of his father and mother.

For Dick Box was really Dick Sanden, and the mystery of his identity was solved.

What a happy time followed, and how fervent were the thanks poured out on Mr. Crosscrab for his part in the affair I leave my young readers to imagine.

"I remember it all now," said Dick after he had talked with his parents and many things had been explained.

"All but how you came to wander off and sleep in that box," said his mother with a smile.

"I think I can explain that," said Mr. Crosscrab. "I made some inquiries at the Grand Central Station to-day. It appears that on the day Dick was to start for Chicago there was an accident. A boy waiting on the platform to take a train was hit on the head by a trunk which fell from the top of a pile on a truck. The boy was knocked unconscious, and an ambulance was summoned to take him to the hospital. The ambulance doctor temporarily dressed the boy's injury and placed him in the vehicle, together with a valise the boy had with him.

"The start was made for the hospital. On the way the ambulance had to stop because of a blockade on account of a fire. The doctor left his place at the rear of the vehicle to see if there was any need of his services, for there was a rumor some one had been burned in the blaze, and when he came back his boy patient was gone. And from that time to this the authorities never heard anything about him. They concluded he had not been badly hurt, and had slipped out of the ambulance and run away, not being noticed in the crowd. The valise was also gone, and from the fact that Dick did not have it when he awoke in the box, it was probably stolen."

"And I guess that's what happened," said Dick's father. "The valise contained Dick's tickets and most of his money. He probably partly regained his senses in the ambulance, slipped out and wandered around, half dazed, forgetting all about himself, until he found the box and went to sleep in it."

"My poor boy!" said his mother, unable to keep back the tears. "What a terrible time you had! Oh, how worried we were when we got back from Europe and found your cousin knew nothing about you!"

"Yes, you must have worried, mother," said Dick, "but I got along pretty well. Jimmy and I have built up a fine business. I'm almost sorry I can't stay and help him buy that stand."

"Don't let that worry you, my son," said Mr. Sanden with a smile and a hearty hand-clasp for Jimmy. "I'll see that your partner has the finest stand in New York."

"Crimps!" exclaimed Jimmy, forgetting himself under the excitement of the occasion. "Dat'll be bul—I mean that will be fine!"

And so it turned out. Mr. Sanden was a wealthy man, more so than ever since coming into the European property, and Jimmy was made proprietor of one of the largest and finest news-stands in the big city. For fear sharpers might take advantage of him, Mr. Crosscrab and Mr. Snowden agreed to look after certain matters for him.

"But I won't have any partner," said Jimmy, when details had been arranged about the stand, and arrangements made for Dick and his parents to go home.

"Yes, you will," said Dick with a smile. "Frank Merton is going to be your partner, and Sam Schmidt will be general assistant."

Thus it was arranged, and to-day those newsboy partners, (the three of them, for Sam was given a share in the business) do a large business in papers and magazines.

As for Dick Box—I mean Dick Sanden—he went back to Slaterville, where many friends whom he had forgotten for a short period were very glad to see him. He often comes to New York now, for he has grown to be quite a man, and he never forgets to visit Jimmy, Frank and Sam, who are now useful and respected citizens. So, you see, the misfortune which came to our hero was the means of good to several, and the little partnership started between Jimmy and Dick had a far-reaching result.

THE END

Made in the USA
Monee, IL
27 September 2023

43532986R00052